ALFRED HITCHCOCK'S

Sinister Spies

Random House 🏠 New York

The editor wishes to thank the following for permission to reprint:

Arkham House for "The Strange Drug of Dr. Caber" from *The Fourth Book of Jorkens*, Copyright, 1948, by Lord Dunsany.

Campbell Thomson & McLaughlin Limited for "The Army of the Shadows," Copyright 1939 by Eric Ambler.

The Estate of the late W. Somerset Maugham, William Heinemann Ltd., and Doubleday and Company, Inc., for "The Traitor," from *Ashenden*, copyright 1927 by W. Somerset Maugham.

Curtis Brown, Ltd. for "Code No. 2," by Edgar Wallace, © Copyright, 1966, by Edgar Wallace Limited.

The author and the author's agents, Scott Meredith Literary Agency, Inc., 845 Third Avenue, New York, New York 10022, for "The Problem Solver and the Spy," by Christopher Anvil, © Copyright, 1965, by Davis Publications, Inc. Appeared first in *Ellery Queen's Mystery Magazine*.

Curtis Brown, Ltd. for "The Uninvited" by Michael Gilbert, © Copyright 1960, by Popular Publications, Inc.

Curtis Brown, Ltd. for "QL696.C9" by Anthony Boucher, Copyright 1943, by Anthony Boucher.

Curtis Brown, Ltd. and Patricia McGerr for "Legacy of Danger," © Copyright, 1963, by United Newspapers Magazine Corporation.

Abby Sheckley for "Citizen in Space," by Robert Sheckley, © Copyright, 1955, by HMH Publishing Co., Inc.

The editor gratefully acknowledges the invaluable assistance of Robert Arthur in the preparation of this volume.

First paperback edition (abridged) published in 1982.

Library of Congress Cataloging in Publication Data

Main entry under title: Alfred Hitchcock's sinister spies. SUMMARY: A collection of short stories involving the daring of spies and counterspies. 1. Spy stories. 2. Children's stories, English. 3. Children's stories, American. [1. Spies—Fiction. 2. Short stories] I. Hitchcock, Alfred, 1899–1980. PZ5.A358937 1982 813′.0872′08 [Fic] 82–3703 AACR2 ISBN: 0–394–84901–9

Manufactured in the United States of America 1 2 3 4 5 6 7 8 9 0

Contents

Spies and Otherwise

Ssssh! Don't look now, but you're being spied on. You don't know it, but you are. Who's doing it? It's not a who, it's a what.

See that big, dark eye in the corner staring at you? See how it seems to watch your movements without ever blinking, no matter where you are in the room? That's what's spying on you.

Oh, it's just your television set? Well—maybe. But did it ever occur to you that when you're not looking at it, it's looking at you? Who's to say that all those characters you watch night after night don't watch *you* when the set is off? The idea is a little unsettling, isn't it? Maybe you'll want to be more careful about what you do when the TV set is looking at you.

To turn to a more serious note, we live in an age of espionage. Life today is so complicated and new developments take place so fast that it is vital for many nations to know what other nations are doing or planning. So the international spy has multiplied a thousandfold. Scientists or street sweepers may act as spies, for money, for patriotism or adventure.

But though the work of spies is deadly serious, their adventures can be suspenseful entertainment. In this volume I have assembled for you some stories—fiction, all of them—of spying and counterspying, of espionage and danger. I hope you will enjoy them for what they are—tales of excitement and adventure. They cover the whole period from World War I right up to the day after the day after tomorrow.

Have fun with them!

ALFRED HITCHCOCK

P.S.   I didn't really mean it about your TV set watching you. It isn't—at least, not yet.

The Strange Drug of Dr. Caber

Lord Dunsany

We had got on to a rather commonplace topic one day at the Billiards Club, though why it is of so much public interest as to have become commonplace I do not quite know; but we were discussing murder, and how to do it successfully. Some argued that it was easy, and some hard, but I need not go over the arguments. Suffice it to say that the hard school were winning, and it was about to be accepted by the Club that murder cannot successfully be committed, when Jorkens joined in.

"I think I may have mentioned to you some time or other," he said, "a man I once knew called Dr. Caber. He's no longer practicing now, poor fellow, and perhaps there is no harm in mentioning that he did a very successful murder. Of course the kind of thing was in his line. I don't mean that he was a murderer, I wouldn't say that of him; but he was a good deal in with people who were, and some of them often came to him for help; and being one of the most inventive geniuses of his time, he was able to help them in a number of ways. I think I told you one. Getting them out of their trouble after they had got into it was his line. But on this occasion they wanted something new, and Caber said he would have nothing to do with it, as it was against his principles, and of course wholly illegal. So they raised their price, and Caber was still against it, but said he would do it merely to oblige them."

"Do what?" asked Terbut.

"I'll tell you," said Jorkens. "There was a fellow with a perfect English accent, correct papers, and a good reason for being in England. One of the dangerous sort. One man said he was a German, and had to pay heavy damages. Norman Smith was his name. Well, this man Smith had a motor-bicycle, and traveled about the roads a good deal, especially where there were aerodromes, and got to know a good deal without leaving the road or doing anything really suspicious; and one day he got to know a secret about aeroplanes in a certain district, which was about the most dangerous secret he could have got hold of. It was sometime in the year 1938."

"What planes were those?" asked Terbut.

"There weren't any," said Jorkens. "That was the deadly secret. We didn't even know it ourselves, bar a very few. Over a large area in the East of England there were no planes at all, and only a very few available to be sent there. If he had got that secret home to where he really came from, they would have known that they had us at their mercy; the mercy, that is to say, of the gentry that ran Belsen. Well, the Government were informed, but they were busy with several other things; so the people who were watching Norman Smith decided to go to Caber; and Caber, as I told you, refused to help them, but in the end they talked him round. Well, first of all Caber asked for all the facts; and then he sat silent a long time, smoking some kind of a pipe carved out of an Indian tree; and then he told them his wonderful plan, or as much of it as he thought it necessary for them to know.

"We weren't entirely blind or deaf in those days, and Smith was watched all right, and his letters were watched; but what they couldn't guard against was his going back to Germany and heiling Hitler and telling them by word of mouth where we had no defenses. Unfortunately he took no interest in the defenses we had; he could have been arrested if he had pried into them. But Norman Smith knew how to keep inside our law. My friends of course were outside it, and he wasn't quite looking for them; not that he didn't take precautions of every sort, and his principal precaution was a huge Alsatian, about which they told Caber, a good savage dog of the old Belsen breed, the kind that German ladies used to use to keep the female prisoners in order.

"Well, Norman Smith had a house in Hertford-shire, and there he kept his Alsatian, just in case any lawless people should try to get in at night. Caber asked so many questions about this savage dog that my friends got the idea that he meant to poison it, and one of them even hinted that so simple a plan was hardly worth the money. But it was foolish of them to suppose that one of the greatest masters of the underworld would hold his position there by making plans so simple that any little dog-stealer could have competed with him. Nor was it easy to poison the dog, for Norman Smith had him guarded by two or three cur dogs, as destroyers guard a battleship. The dog was the crux of the whole situation, and there seemed no way of getting by him at night, and my friends were not going about very much by day at that time. Among the facts they told Caber was that Norman Smith used every now and then to go to the seaside and stay in a large hotel. It is strange how fond spies always are of the sea.

" 'You'll have to do it there,' said Caber at last. 'He won't be able to have the dog in the hotel.'

" 'But we won't be able to get in either,' said my friends. 'They'll have a hall porter and waiters, if they don't have the dog.'

" 'Then you'll have to do it by day, when he's out for a walk,' said Caber.

" 'We don't like that kind of thing by daylight,' said one of them.

"Caber looked at them. 'You don't know what kind of thing yet,' he said.

" 'Well, what is it?' they asked.

" 'Two or three men to follow him,' said Caber, 'a little fracas, and a jab with a small needle.'

" 'I don't like poison,' said one of them. 'It can always be traced.'

"Caber opened his eyes wide. 'My friends,' he said, 'am I a child?'

" 'I don't care, it can always be traced,' said the other man, still sticking to his point.

" 'But I am not going to give you any poison,' said Caber.

" 'Well, what's the use of the needle?' they asked.

" 'The slightest jab,' said Caber, 'a little harmless fluid put in with a syringe, then your two men get away; better have three. And after that, he brings a charge of assault, and the police look for the men. But so long as no harm comes to Norman Smith, and the police have only his word that he was pricked by a needle, it is only a local affair, not Scotland Yard and the police of the countryside, as it would be in the case of a murder.'

" 'Not murder, of course, exactly,' said one of my friends. 'But, then, what is going to be the effect of your needle and syringe?'

" 'Nothing whatever,' said Caber. 'You had better do it at the beginning of his trip to the sea, so as to give plenty of time for them to see the whole thing is innocuous.'

" 'Then, what is the use of it?' they asked bluntly.

" 'Merely,' said Caber, 'that when he goes home, or very soon after, he will accidentally die.'

" 'They'll trace a thing like that,' said the man who didn't like poison.

" 'How do you like my little room?' said Caber. 'I've had it a long time. I've got to like it myself. But what do you think of it?'

" 'What's that got to do with our business?' asked the other.

" 'Only,' said Caber, 'that if things I did had ever been traced, perhaps I shouldn't be here. I don't say I shouldn't; but I might have moved before now.'

"And somehow that seemed to silence them. And then one said, 'You told us it was innocuous.'

" 'Entirely,' said Caber.

" 'But the man would die when he went home.'

" 'Certainly,' Caber said.

" 'Then I don't quite see . . .

" 'Perhaps we had better leave it to Dr. Caber,' said one of the others.

"And that in the end was what they did. Well, Norman Smith went to the sea sure enough in a week-or-so's time, and stayed at the large hotel, and left a man in Hertfordshire to feed his dangerous dog, and the three little yapping dogs that were to look after it. And the first morning after he arrived at the sea Norman Smith went for a walk, and he got into a bit of a row with three men near some golf-links, and he went to the police complaining he had been assaulted and alleging he had been impregnated or inoculated with some deadly disease or poison. He had a pinprick to show on his arm, and he asserted that near it he had seen a drop of some liquid that had a sweaty smell. And the police sent for two doctors, who made tests and examinations, all of which proved that Smith was perfectly fit. By the end of a week the whole thing had blown over, so far as the police were concerned, and nothing was traced to anybody. You see, poisons can always be traced, and bacterial things even easier, because they are rarer, and as for any unknown poison, that's rarest of all, and the police would soon get on to it."

"And what happened?" we asked.

"Norman Smith went home to Hertfordshire," replied Jorkens, "invigorated by his stay by the sea, and cheered by whatever information spies get when they go to the seaside. And that night his Alsatian killed him."

"Yes, a successful murder," said Terbut, "if you can call a dog a murderer."

And one of us said rather diffidently that he didn't quite see how Caber came into it.

"It was a very subtle drug," said Jorkens. "Perfectly harmless, as Caber said. But it changed his smell. It gave him an entirely new scent. Of course no Alsatian dog would put up with a thing like that."

The Army of the Shadows

Eric Ambler

It is three years since Llewellyn removed my appendix; but we still meet occasionally. I am dimly related to his wife: that, at least, is the pretext for the acquaintanceship. The truth is that, during my convalescence, we happened to discover that we both like the same musicians. Before the war we usually met when there was some Sibelius being played and went to hear it together. I was a little puzzled when, about three weeks ago, he telephoned with the suggestion that I should dine at his house that night. There was not, I knew, a concert of any sort in London. I agreed, however, to grope my way round to Upper Wimpole Street shortly before eight o'clock.

It was not until he had presented me with a brandy that I found out why I had been invited to dinner.

"Do you remember," he said suddenly, "that I spent a week or so in Belgrade last year? I missed Beecham doing the Second through it. There was one of those international medical bun fights being held there, and I went to represent the Association. My German is fairly good, you know. I motored. Can't stick trains. Anyway, on the way back a very funny thing happened to me. Did I ever tell you about it?"

"I don't think so."

"I thought not. Well"—he laughed self-consciously—"it was so funny now there's a war on that I've been amusing myself by writing the whole thing down. I wondered whether you'd be good enough to cast a professional eye over it for me. I've tried"—he laughed again—"to make a really literary job of it. Like a story, you know."

His hand had been out of sight behind the arm of his chair, but now it emerged from hiding holding a wad of typewritten sheets.

"It's typed," he said, planking it down on my knees. And then, with a theatrical glance at his watch, "Good Lord, it's ten. There's a telephone call I must make. Excuse me for a minute or two, will you?"

He was out of the room before I could open my mouth to reply. I was left alone with the manuscript.

I picked it up. It was entitled "A Strange Encounter." With a sigh, I turned over the title page and began, rather irritably, to read:

The Stelvio Pass is snowed up in winter, and towards the end of November most sensible men driving to Paris from Belgrade or beyond take the long way round via Milan rather than risk being stopped by an early fall of snow. But I was in a hurry and took a chance. By the time I reached Bolzano I was sorry I had done so. It was bitterly cold, and the sky ahead was leaden. At Merano I seriously considered turning back. Instead, I pushed on as hard as I could go. If I had had any sense I should have stopped for petrol before I started the really serious part of the climb. I had six gallons by the gauge then. I knew that it wasn't accurate, but I had filled up early that morning and calculated that I had enough to get me to Sargans. In my anxiety to beat the snow I overlooked the fact that I had miles of low-gear driving to do. On the Swiss side and on the Sargans road where it runs within a mile or two of the Rhätikon part of the German frontier, the car spluttered to a standstill.

For a minute or two I sat there swearing at and to myself and wondering what on earth I was going to do. I was, I knew, the only thing on the road that night for miles.

It was about eight o'clock, very dark and very cold. Except for the faint creaking of the cooling engine and the rustle of the breeze in some nearby trees, there wasn't a sound to be heard. Ahead, the road in the headlights curved away to the right. I got out the map and tried to find out where I was.

I had passed through one village since I left Klosters, and I knew that it was about ten kilometers back. I must, therefore, either walk back ten kilometers to that village, or forward to the next village, whichever was the nearer. I looked at the map. It was of that useless kind that they sell to motorists. There was nothing marked between Klosters and Sargans. For all I knew, the next village might be fifteen or twenty kilometers away.

An Alpine road on a late November night is not the place to choose if you want to sleep in your car. I decided to walk back the way I had come.

I had a box of those small Italian waxed matches with me when I started out. There were, I thought, about a hundred in the box, and I calculated that, if I struck one every hundred meters, they would last until I reached the village.

That was when I was near the lights of the car. When I got out of sight of them, things were different. The darkness seemed to press against the backs of my eyes. It was almost painful. I could not even see the shape of the road along which I was walking. It was only by the rustling and the smell of resin that I knew that I was walking between fir trees. By the time I had covered a mile I had six matches left. Then it began to snow.

I say "snow." It had been snow; but the Sargans road was still below the snow-line, and the stuff came down as a sort of half-frozen mush that slid down my face into the gap between my coat collar and my neck.

I must have done about another mile and a half when the real trouble began. I still had the six matches, but my hands were too numb to get them out of the box without wetting them, and I had been going forward blindly, sometimes on the road and sometimes off it. I was wondering whether I would get along better if I sang, when I walked into a telegraph post.

It was of pre-cast concrete and the edge was as

sharp as a razor. My face was as numb as my hands and I didn't feel much except a sickening jar; but I could taste blood trickling between my teeth and found that my nose was bleeding. It was as I held my head back to stop it that I saw the light, looking for all the world as if it were suspended in mid-air above me.

It wasn't suspended in mid-air, and it wasn't above me. Darkness does strange things to perspective. After a few seconds I saw that it was showing through the trees on the hillside, up off the right of the road.

Anyone who has been in the sort of mess that I was in will know exactly how my mind worked at that moment. I did not speculate as to the origin of that God-forsaken light or as to whether or not the owner of it would be pleased to see me. I was cold and wet, my nose was bleeding, and I would not have cared if someone had told me that behind the light was a maniac with a machine gun. I knew only that the light meant there was some sort of human habitation near me and that I was going to spend the night in it.

I moved over to the other side of the road and began to feel my way along the wire fence I found there. Twenty yards or so farther on, my hands touched a wooden gate. The light was no longer visible, but I pushed the gate open and walked on into the blackness.

The ground rose steeply under my feet. It was a path of sorts, and soon I stumbled over the beginnings of a flight of log steps. There must have been well over a hundred of them. Then there was another stretch of path, not quite so steep. When I again saw the light, I was only about twenty yards from it.

It came from an oil reading-lamp standing near a window. From the shape of the window and the reflected light of the lamp, I could see that the place was a small chalet of the kind usually let to families for the summer season or for the winter sports. That it should be occupied at the end of November was curious. But I didn't ponder over the curiosity: I had seen something else through the window besides the lamp. The light from a fire was flickering in the room.

I went forward up the path to the door. There was no knocker. I hammered on the wet, varnished wood with my fist and waited. There was no sound from inside. After a moment or two I knocked again. Still there was no sign of life within. I knocked and waited for several minutes. Then I began to shiver. In desperation I grabbed the latch of the door and rattled it violently. The next moment I felt it give and the door creaked open a few inches.

I think that I have a normal, healthy respect for the property and privacy of my fellow-creatures; but at that moment I was feeling neither normal nor healthy. Obviously, the owner of the chalet could not be far away. I stood there for a moment or two, hesitating. I could smell the wood smoke from the fire, and mingled with it a bitter, oily smell which seemed faintly familiar. But all I cared about was the fire. I hesitated no longer and walked in.

As soon as I was inside I saw that there was something more than curious about the place, and that I should have waited.

The room itself was ordinary enough. It was rather larger than I had expected, but there were the usual pinewood walls, the usual pinewood floor, the usual pinewood staircase up to the bedrooms, and the usual tiled fireplace. There were the usual tables and chairs, too: turned and painted nonsense of the kind that sometimes finds its way into English tea shops. There were red gingham curtains over the windows. You felt that the owner probably had lots of other places just like it, and that he made a good thing out of letting them.

No, it was what had been added to the room that was curious. All the furniture had been crowded into one half of the space. In the other half, standing on linoleum and looking as if it were used a good deal, was a printing press.

The machine was a small treadle platen of the kind used by jobbing printers for running off tradesmen's circulars. It looked very old and decrepit. Alongside it on a trestle table were a case of type and a small proofing press with a locked-up form in it. On a second table stood a pile of interleaved sheets, beside which was a stack of what appeared to be some of the same sheets folded. The folding was obviously being done by hand. I picked up one of the folded sheets.

It looked like one of those long, narrow business-promotion folders issued by travel agencies. The front page was devoted to the reproduction, in watery blue ink, of a lino-cut of a clump of pines on the shore of a lake, and the display of the name "TITISEE." Page two and the page folded in to face it carried a rhapsodical account in German of the beauties of Baden in general and Lake Titisee in particular.

I put the folder down. An inaccessible Swiss chalet was an odd place to choose for printing German travel advertisements; but I was not disposed to dwell on its oddity. I was cold.

I was moving towards the fire when my eye was caught by five words printed in bold capitals on one of the unfolded sheets on the table: "DEUTSCHE MÄNNER UND FRAUEN, KAMERA-DEN!"

I stood still. I remember that my heart thudded against my ribs as suddenly and violently as it had earlier that day on the Stelvio when some crazy fool in a Hispano had nearly crowded me off the road.

I leaned forward, picked the folder up again, and opened it right out. The message began on the second of the three inside pages.

"GERMAN MEN AND WOMEN, COMRADES! We speak to you with the voice of German Democracy, bringing you news. Neither Nazi propaganda nor the Gestapo can silence us, for we have an ally which is proof against floggings, an ally which no man in the history of the world has been able to defeat. That ally is Truth. Hear then, people of Germany, the Truth which is concealed from you. Hear it, remember it, and repeat it. The sooner the Truth is known, the sooner will Germany again hold up its head among the free nations of the world."

Then followed a sort of news bulletin consisting of facts and figures (especially figures) about the economic condition of Germany. There was also news of a strike in the Krupp works at Essen and a short description of a riot outside a shipyard in Hamburg.

I put it down again. Now I knew why these "travel advertisements" were being printed in an inaccessible Swiss chalet instead of in Germany itself. No German railway official would distribute these folders. That business would be left to more desperate men. These folders would not collect dust on the counters of travel agencies. They would be found in trains and in trams, in buses and in parked cars, in waiting rooms and in bars, under restaurant plates and inside table napkins. Some of the men that put them there would be caught and tortured to betray their fellows; but the distribution would go on. The folders would be read, perhaps furtively discussed. A little more truth would seep through Goebbels' dam of lies to rot still further the creaking foundation of Nazidom.

Then, as I stood there with the smell of wood smoke and printing ink in my nostrils, as I stood staring at that decrepit little machine as if it were the very voice of freedom, I heard footsteps outside.

I suppose that I should have stood my ground. I had, after all, a perfectly good explanation of my presence there. My car and the blood from my nose would confirm my story. But I didn't reason that way. I had stumbled on a secret, and my first impulse was to try to hide the fact from the owner of the secret. I obeyed that impulse.

I looked around quickly and saw the stairs. Before I had even begun to wonder if I might not be doing something excessively stupid, I was up the stairs and opening the first door I came to on the landing. In the half-light I caught a glimpse of a bed; then I was inside the room with the door slightly ajar. I could see across the landing and through the wooden palings along it to the top of the window at the far side of the room below.

I knew that someone had come in: I could hear him moving about. He lit another lamp. There was a sound from the door and a second person entered.

A woman's voice said in German, "Thank God, Johann has left a good fire."

There was an answering grunt. It came from the man. I could almost feel them warming their hands.

"Get the coffee, Freda," said the man suddenly. "I must go back soon."

"But Bruno is there. You should take a little rest first."

"Bruno is a Berliner. He is not as used to the cold as I am. If Kurt should come now he would be tired. Bruno could only look after himself."

There was silence for a moment. Then the woman spoke again.

"Do you really think that he will come now, Stephan? It is so late." She paused. Her voice had sounded casual, elaborately casual; but now, as she went on, there was an edge to it that touched the nerves. "I can keep quite calm about it, you see, Stephan. I wish to believe, but it is so late, isn't it? You don't think he will come now, do you? Admit it."

He laughed, but too heartily. "You are too nervous, Freda. Kurt can take care of himself. He knows all the tricks now. He may have been waiting for the first snow. The frontier guards would not be so alert on a night like this."

"He should have been back a week ago. You know that as well as I do, Stephan. He has never been delayed so long before. They have got him. That is all. You see, I can be calm about it even though he is my dear husband." And then her voice broke. "I knew it would happen sooner or later. I knew it. First Hans, then Karl, and now Kurt. Those swine, those—"

She sobbed and broke suddenly into passionate weeping. He tried helplessly to comfort her.

I had heard enough. I was shaking from head to foot; but whether it was the cold or not, I don't know. I stood back from the door. Then, as I did so, I heard a sound from behind me.

I had noticed the bed as I had slipped into the room, but the idea that there might be someone in it had not entered my head. Now, as I whipped around, I saw that I had made a serious mistake.

Sitting on the edge of the bed in which he had been lying was a very thin, middle-aged man in a nightshirt. By the faint light from the landing I could see his eyes, bleary from sleep, and his grizzled hair standing ludicrously on end. But for one thing I should have laughed. That one thing was the large automatic pistol which he held pointed at me. His hand was as steady as a rock.

"Don't move," he said. He raised his voice. "Stephan! Come quickly!"

"I must apologize . . ." I began in German.

"You will be allowed to speak later."

I heard Stephan dash up the stairs.

"What is it, Johann?"

"Come here."

The door was pushed open behind me. I heard him draw in his breath sharply.

"Who is it?"

"I do not know. I was awakened by a noise. I was about to get up when this man came into the room. He did not see me. He has been listening to your conversation. He must have been examining the plant when he heard you returning."

"If you will allow me to explain . . ." I began.

"You may explain downstairs," said the man called Stephan. "Give me the pistol, Johann."

The pistol changed hands and I could see Stephan, a lean, rawboned fellow with broad, sharp shoulders and dangerous eyes. He wore black oilskins and gum boots. I saw the muscles in his cheeks tighten.

"Raise your hands and walk downstairs. Slowly. If you run, I shall shoot immediately. March."

I went downstairs.

The woman, Freda, was standing by the door, staring blankly up at me as I descended. She must have been about thirty and had that soft rather

matronly look about her that is characteristic of so
many young German women. She was short and
plump, and as if to accentuate the fact, her straw-
colored hair was plaited across her head. Wisps of
the hair had become detached and clung wetly to
the sides of her neck. She too wore a black oilskin
coat and gum boots.

The gray eyes, red and swollen with crying,
looked beyond me.

"Who is it, Stephan?"

"He was hiding upstairs."

We had reached the foot of the stairs. He mo-
tioned me away from the door and towards the
fire. "Now, we will hear your explanation."

I gave it with profuse apologies. I admitted that I
had examined the folders and read one. "It seemed
to me," I concluded, "that my presence might be
embarrassing to you. I was about to leave when
you returned. Then, I am afraid, I lost my head and
attempted to hide."

Not one of them was believing a word that I was
saying: I could see that from their faces. "I assure
you," I went on in exasperation, "that what I am
telling . . ."

"What nationality are you?"

"British. I . . ."

"Then speak English. What were you doing on
this road?"

"I am on my way home from Belgrade. I crossed
the Yugoslav frontier yesterday and the Italian
frontier at Stelvio this afternoon. My passport was
stamped at both places if you wish to . . ."

"Why were you in Belgrade?"

"I am a surgeon. I have been attending an international medical convention there."

"Let me see your passport, please."

"Certainly. I have . . ." And then with my hand in my inside pocket, I stopped. My heart felt as if it had come right into my throat. In my haste to be away after the Italian Customs had finished with me, I had thrust my passport with the Customs carnet for the car into the pocket beside me on the door of the car.

They were watching me with expressionless faces. Now, as my hand reappeared empty, I saw Stephan raise his pistol.

"Well?"

"I am sorry." Like a fool I had begun to speak in German again. "I find that I have left my passport in my car. It is several kilometers along the road. If . . ."

And then the woman burst out as if she couldn't stand listening to me any longer.

"Don't you see? Don't you see?" she cried. "It is quite clear. They have found out that we are here. Perhaps after all these months Hans or Karl has been tortured by them into speaking. And so they have taken Kurt and sent this man to spy upon us. It is clear. Don't you see?"

She turned suddenly, and I thought she was going to attack me. Then Stephan put his hand on her arm.

"Gently, Freda." He turned to me again, and his expression hardened. "You see, my friend, what is in our minds? We know our danger, you see. The fact that we are in Swiss territory will not protect us if the Gestapo should trace us. The Nazis, we know, have little respect for frontiers. The Gestapo have none. They would murder us here as confidently as they would if we were in the Third Reich. We do not underrate their cunning. The fact that you are not a German is not conclusive. You may be what you say you are: you may not. If you are, so much the better. If not, then, I give you fair warning, you will be shot. You say that your passport is in your car several kilometers along the road. Unfortunately, it is not possible for us to spare time tonight to see if that is true. Nor is it possible for one of us to stand guard over you all night. You have already disturbed the first sleep Johann has had in twenty-four hours. There is only one thing for it, I'm afraid. It is undignified and barbaric; but I see no other way. We shall be forced to tie you up so that you cannot leave."

"But this is absurd," I cried angrily. "Good heavens, man, I realize that I've only myself to blame for being here; but surely you could have the common decency to . . ."

"The question," he said sternly, "is not of decency, but of necessity. We have no time tonight for six-kilometer walks. One of our comrades has been delivering a consignment of these folders to our friends in Germany. We hope and believe that he will return to us across the frontier tonight. He may need our help. Mountaineering in such weather is exhausting. Freda, get me some of the cord we use for tying the packages."

I wanted to say something, but the words would not come. I was too angry. I don't think that I've ever been so angry in my life before.

She brought the cord. It was thick gray stuff. He took it and gave the pistol to Johann. Then he came towards me.

I don't think they liked the business any more than I did. He had gone a bit white and he wouldn't look me in the eyes. I think that I must have been white myself, but it was anger with me. He put the cord under one of my elbows. I snatched it away.

"You had better submit," he said harshly.

"To spare your feelings? Certainly not. You'll have to use force, my friend. But don't worry. You'll get used to it. You'll be a good Nazi yet. You should knock me down. That'll make it easier."

What color there was left in his face went. A good deal of my anger evaporated at that moment. I felt sorry for the poor devil. I really believe that I should have let him tie me up. But I never knew for certain, for at that moment there was an interruption.

It was the woman who heard it first—the sound of someone running up the path outside. The next moment a man burst wildly into the room.

Stephan had turned. "Bruno! What is it? Why aren't you at the hut?"

The man was striving to get his breath, and for a moment he could hardly speak. His face above the streaming oilskins was blue with cold. Then he gasped out.

"Kurt! He is at the hut! He is wounded—badly!"

The woman gave a little whimpering cry and

her hands went to her face. Stephan gripped the newcomer's shoulder.

"What has happened? Quickly!"

"It was dark. The Swiss did not see him. It was one of our patrols. They shot him when he was actually on the Swiss side. He was wounded in the thigh. He crawled on to the hut, but he can go no further. He . . ."

But Stephan had ceased to listen. He turned sharply. "Johann, you must dress yourself at once. Bruno, take the pistol and guard this man. He broke in here. He may be dangerous. Freda, get the cognac and the iodine. We shall need them for Kurt."

He himself went to a cupboard and got out some handkerchiefs, which he began tearing feverishly into strips, which he knotted together. Still gasping for breath, the man Bruno had taken the pistol and was staring at me with a puzzled frown. Then the woman reappeared from the kitchen carrying a bottle of cognac and a small tube of iodine of the sort that is sold for dabbing at cut fingers. Stephan stuffed them in his pockets with the knotted handkerchiefs. Then he called up the stairs, "Hurry, Johann. We are ready to leave."

It was more than I could bear. Professional fussiness, I suppose.

"Has any one of you," I asked loudly, "ever dealt with a bullet wound before?"

They stared at me. Then Stephan glanced at Bruno.

"If he moves," he said, "shoot." He raised his voice again. "Johann!"

There was an answering cry of reassurance.

"Has it occurred to you," I persisted, "that even if you get him here alive, which I doubt, as you obviously don't know what you're doing, he will need immediate medical attention? Don't you think that one of you had better go for a doctor? Ah, but of course; the doctor would ask questions about a bullet wound, wouldn't he? The matter would be reported to the police."

"We can look after him," Stephan grunted. "Johann! Hurry!"

"It seems a pity," I said reflectively, "that one brave man should have to die because of his friends' stupidity." And then my calm deserted me. "You fool," I shouted. "Listen to me. Do you want to kill this man? You're going about it the right way. I'm a surgeon, and this is a surgeon's business. Take that cognac out of your pocket. We shan't need it. The iodine too. And those pieces of rag. Have you got two or three clean towels?"

The woman nodded stupidly.

"Then get them, please, and be quick. And you said something about some coffee. Have you a flask for it? Good. Then we shall take that. Put plenty of sugar in it. I want blankets, too. Three will be enough, but they must be kept dry. We shall need a stretcher. Get two poles or broomsticks and two old coats. We can make a stretcher of sorts by putting the poles through the sleeves of them. Take this cord of yours too. It will be useful to make slings for the stretcher. And hurry! The man may be bleeding to death. Is he far away?"

The man was glowering at me. "Four kilometers. In a climbing hut in the hills this side of the frontier." He stepped forward and gripped my arm. "If you are tricking us . . ." he began.

"I'm not thinking about you," I snapped. "I'm thinking about a man who's been crawling along with a bullet in his thigh and a touching faith in his friends. Now get those poles, and hurry."

They hurried. In three minutes they had the things collected. The exhausted Bruno's oilskins and gum boots had, at my suggestion, been transferred to me. Then I tied one of the blankets around my waist under my coat, and told Stephan and Johann to do the same.

"I," said the woman, "will take the other things."

"You," I said, "will stay here, please."

She straightened up at that. "No," she said firmly, "I will come with you. I shall be quite calm. You will see."

"Nevertheless," I said rather brutally, "you will be more useful here. A bed must be ready by the fire here. There must also be hot bricks and plenty of blankets. I shall need, besides, both boiled and boiling water. You have plenty of ordinary salt, I suppose?"

"Yes, *Herr Doktor*. But . . ."

"We are wasting time."

Two minutes later we left.

I shall never forget that climb. It began about half a mile along the road below the chalet. The first part was mostly up narrow paths between trees. They were covered with pine needles and, in the rain, as slippery as the devil. We had been

climbing steadily for about half an hour when
Stephan, who had been leading the way with a
storm lantern, paused.

"I must put out the light here," he said. "The
frontier is only three kilometers from here, and
the guards patrol to a depth of two kilometers.
They must not see us." He blew out the lamp.
"Turn around," he said then. "You will see another light."

I saw it, far away below us, a pinpoint.

"That is our light. When we are returning from
Germany, we can see it from across the frontier
and know that we are nearly home and that our
friends are waiting. Hold on to my coat now. You
need not worry about Johann behind you. He
knows the path well. This way, *Herr Doktor.*"

It was the only sign he gave that he had decided
to accept me for what I said I was.

I cannot conceive of how anyone could know
that path well. The surface soon changed from
pine needles to a sort of rocky rubble, and it
twisted and turned like a wounded snake. The
wind had dropped, but it was colder than ever, and
I found myself crunching through sugary patches
of half-frozen slush. I wondered how on earth we
were going to bring down a wounded man on an
improvised stretcher.

We had been creeping along without the light
for about twenty minutes when Stephan stopped
and, shielding the lamp with his coat, relit it. I
saw that we had arrived.

The climbing hut was built against the side of
an overhanging rock face. It was about six feet

square inside, and the man was lying diagonally across it on his face. There was a large bloodstain on the floor beneath him. He was semi-conscious. His eyes were closed, but he mumbled something as I felt for his pulse.

"Will he live?" whispered Stephan.

I didn't know. The pulse was there, but it was feeble and rapid. His breathing was shallow. I looked at the wound. The bullet had entered on the inner side of the left thigh just below the groin. There was a little bleeding, but it obviously hadn't touched the femoral artery and, as far as I could see, the bone was all right. I made a dressing with one of the towels and tied it in place with another. The bullet could wait. The immediate danger was from shock aggravated by exposure. I got to work with the blankets and the flask of coffee. Soon the pulse strengthened a little, and after about half an hour I told them how to prepare the stretcher.

I don't know how they got him down that path in the darkness. It was all I could do to get down by myself. It was snowing hard now in great fleecy chunks that blinded you when you moved forward. I was prepared for them to slip and drop the stretcher; but they didn't. It was slow work, however, and it was a good forty minutes before we got to the point where it was safe to light the lamp.

After that I was able to help with the stretcher. At the foot of the path up to the chalet, I went ahead with the lantern. The woman heard my footsteps and came to the door. I realized that we must have been gone for the best part of three hours.

"They're bringing him up," I said. "He'll be all right. I shall need your help now."

She said, "The bed is ready." And then, "Is it serious, *Herr Doktor*?"

"No." I didn't tell her then that there was a bullet to be taken out.

It was a nasty job. The wound itself wasn't so bad. The bullet must have been pretty well spent, for it had lodged up against the bone without doing any real damage. It was the instruments that made it difficult. They came from the kitchen. He didn't stand up to it very well, and I wasn't surprised. I didn't feel so good myself when I'd finished. The cognac came in useful after all.

We finally got him to sleep about five.

"He'll be all right now," I said.

The woman looked at me and I saw the tears begin to trickle down her cheeks. It was only then that I remembered that she wasn't a nurse, but his wife.

It was Johann who comforted her. Stephan came over to me.

"We owe you a great debt, *Herr Doktor*," he said. "I must apologize for our behavior earlier this evening. We have not always been savages, you know. Kurt was a professor of zoology. Johann was a master printer. I was an architect. Now we are those who crawl across frontiers at night and plot like criminals. We have been treated like savages, and so we live like them. We forget sometimes that we were civilized. We ask your pardon. I do not know how we can repay you for what you have done. We . . ."

But I was too tired for speeches. I smiled quickly at him.

"All that I need by way of a fee is another glass of cognac and a bed to sleep in for a few hours. I suggest, by the way, that you get a doctor in to look at the patient later today. There will be a little fever to treat. Tell the doctor he fell upon his climbing axe. He won't believe you, but there'll be no bullet for him to be inquisitive about. Oh, and if you could find me a little petrol for my car . . ."

It was five in the afternoon and almost dark again when Stephan woke me. The local doctor, he reported, as he set an enormous tray of food down beside the bed, had been, dressed the wound, prescribed, and gone. My car was filled up with petrol and awaited me below if I wished to drive to Zürich that night. Kurt was awake and could not be prevailed upon to sleep until he had thanked me.

They were all there, grouped about the bed, when I went downstairs. Bruno was the only one who looked as if he had had any sleep.

He sprang to his feet. "Here, Kurt," he said facetiously, "is the *Herr Doktor*. He is going to cut your leg off."

Only the woman did not laugh at the jest. Kurt himself was smiling when I bent over to look at him.

He was a youngish-looking man of about forty with intelligent brown eyes and a high, wide forehead. The smile faded from his face as he looked at me.

"You know what I wish to say, *Herr Doktor*?"

I took refuge in professional brusqueness. "The less you say, the better," I said, and felt for his pulse. But as I did so his fingers moved and gripped my hand.

"One day soon," he said, "England and the Third Reich will be at war. But you will not be at war with Germany. Remember that, please, *Herr Doktor*. Not with Germany. It is people like us who are Germany, and in our way we shall fight with England. You will see."

I left soon after.

At nine that night I was in Zürich.

Llewellyn was back in the room. I put the manuscript down. He looked across at me.

"Very interesting," I said.

"I'd considered sending it up to one of these magazines that publish short stories," he said apologetically. "I thought I'd like your opinion first, though. What do you think?"

I cleared my throat. "Well, of course, it's difficult to say. Very interesting, as I said. But there's no real point to it, is there? It needs something to tie it all together."

"Yes, I see what you mean. It sort of leaves off, doesn't it? But that's how it actually happened." He looked disappointed. "I don't think I could invent an ending. It would be rather a pity, wouldn't it? You see, it's all true."

"Yes, it would be a pity."

"Well, anyway, thanks for reading it. Funny thing to happen. I really only put it down on paper for fun." He got up. "Oh, by the way. I was forgetting. I heard from those people about a week after war broke out. A letter. Let's see now, where did I put it? Ah, yes."

He rummaged in a drawer for a bit, and then tossed a letter over to me.

The envelope bore a Swiss stamp and the postmark was Klosters, September 4th, 1939. The contents felt bulky. I drew them out.

The cause of the bulkiness was what looked like a travel agent's folder doubled up to fit the envelope. I straightened it. On the front page was a lino-cut of a clump of pines on the shore of a lake and the name "TITISEE." I opened out the folder.

"GERMAN MEN AND WOMEN, COMRADES!" The type was worn and battered. "Hitler has led you into war. He fed you with lies about the friendly Polish people. In your name he has now committed a wanton act of aggression against them. As a consequence, the free democracies of England and France have declared war against Germany. Comrades, right and justice are on their side. It is Hitler and National Socialism who are the enemies of peace in Europe. Our place as true Germans is at the side of the democracies against Hitler, against National Socialism. Hitler cannot win this war. But the people of Germany must act. All Germans, Catholics, Protestants, and Jews, must act now. Our Czech and Slovak friends are already refusing to make guns for Hitler. Let us stand by their sides. Remember . . ."

I was about to read on when I saw that the letter which accompanied the folder had fluttered to the carpet. I picked it up. It consisted of a few typewritten lines on an otherwise blank sheet of paper.

"Greetings, *Herr Doktor.* We secured your address from the Customs carnet in your car and write now to wish you good luck. Kurt, Stephan, and Bruno have made many journeys since we saw you and returned safely each time. Today, Kurt leaves again. We pray for him as always. With this letter we send you Johann's newest work so that you shall see that Kurt spoke the truth to you. We are of the army of the shadows. We do not fight for you against our countrymen; but we fight with you against National Socialism, our common enemy.

"*Auf Wiedersehen.*
"FREDA, KURT, STEPHAN, JOHANN, AND BRUNO."

Llewellyn put my glass down on the table beside me. "Help yourself to a cigarette. What do you think of that? Nice of them, wasn't it?" he added. "Sentimental lot, these Germans."

"Somewhere in France"

Richard Harding Davis

Marie Gessler, known as Marie Chaumontel, Jeanne d'Avrechy, the Countess d'Aurillac, was German. Her father, who served through the Franco-Prussian War, was a German spy. It was from her mother she learned to speak French sufficiently well to satisfy even an Academician and, among Parisians, to pass as one. Both her parents were dead. Before they departed, knowing they could leave their daughter nothing save their debts, they had her trained as a nurse. But when they were gone, Marie played politics in the Berlin hospitals, intrigued, indiscriminately misused the appealing, violet eyes. There was a scandal; several scandals. At the age of twenty-five she was dismissed from the Municipal Hospital, and traveled to Monte Carlo. There she met Henri Ravignac, a captain in the French Aviation Corps, who, when his leave ended, escorted her to Paris.

The duties of Captain Ravignac kept him in barracks near the aviation field, but he established Marie in his apartments on the Boulevard Haussmann. One day he brought from the barracks a roll of blueprints, and as he was locking them in a drawer, said: "The Germans would pay through the nose for those!" The remark was indiscreet, but then Marie had told him she was French, and anyone would have believed her.

The next morning the same spirit of adventure that had exiled her from the Berlin hospitals carried her with the blueprints to the German embassy. There, greatly shocked, they first wrote down her name and address, and then, indignant at her proposition, ordered her out. But the day following a strange young German who was not at all indignant, but, on the contrary, quite charming, called upon Marie. For the blueprints he offered her a very large sum, which she accepted. That same hour Marie departed for Berlin. Marie did not need the money. Nor did the argument that she was serving her country greatly impress her. It was rather that she loved intrigue. And so she became a spy.

Henri Ravignac, the man she had robbed of the blueprints, was tried by court-martial. The charge was treason, but Charles Ravignac, his younger brother, promised to prove that the guilty one was the girl, and to that end obtained leave of absence and spent much time and money. At the trial he was able to show the record of Marie in Berlin and Monte Carlo; that she was the daughter of a German secret agent; that on the afternoon the prints disappeared, Marie had left Paris for Berlin. In consequence of this the charge of selling military secrets was altered to one of "gross neglect," and Henri Ravignac was sentenced to two years in the military prison at Tours. But he was of an ancient and noble family, and when they came to take him from his cell in the Cherche-Midi, he was dead. Charles, his brother, disappeared. It was said he also had killed himself; that he had been appointed a military attaché in South America; that to revenge his brother he had entered the secret service; but whatever became of him no one knew. All that was certain was that, thanks to the act of Marie Gessler, on the rolls of the French army the ancient and noble name of Ravignac no longer appeared.

In her chosen profession Marie Gessler found nothing discreditable. Of herself her opinion was not high, and her opinion of men was lower. For her smiles she had watched several sacrifice honor, duty, loyalty; and she held them and their kind in contempt. To lie, to cajole, to rob men of secrets they thought important, and of secrets the importance of which they did not even guess, was to her merely an intricate and exciting game.

She played it very well. So well that in the service her advance was rapid. On important missions she was sent to Russia, through the Balkans; even to the United States. There, with credentials as an army nurse, she inspected military hospitals and unobtrusively asked many innocent questions.

When she begged to be allowed to work in her beloved Paris, "they" told her when the war came "they" intended to plant her inside that city, and that, until then, the less Paris knew of her the better.

But just before the World War broke, she was sent to Rome, to report on which way Italy might jump, and it was not until September that she was recalled. The telegram informed her that her Aunt Elizabeth was ill, and that she must return to Berlin at once. This, she learned from the code book wrapped under the cover of her thermos bottle, meant that she was to report to the general commanding the German forces at Soissons.

From Italy she passed through Switzerland, and, after leaving Basle, was rushed north on military trains to Luxemburg, and then west to Laon. She was accompanied by her companion, Bertha, an elderly and respectable, even distinguished-looking female. In the secret service her number was 528. Their passes from the war office described them as nurses of the German Red Cross. Only the Intelligence Department knew their real mission. With her also, as her chauffeur, was a young Italian soldier of fortune, Paul Anfossi. He had served in the Belgian Congo, in the French Foreign Legion in Algiers, and spoke all the European languages. In Rome, where as a wireless operator he was serving a commercial company, Marie had found him useful, and when war came she obtained for him, from the Wilhelmstrasse, the number 292. From Laon, in one of the automobiles of the General Staff, the three spies were driven first to Soissons, and then, along the road to Meaux and Paris, to the village of Neufchelles. They arrived at midnight, and in a château of one of the champagne princes found the colonel commanding the Intelligence Bureau. He accepted their credentials, destroyed them, and replaced them with a *laisser-passer* signed by the mayor of Laon. That dignitary, the colonel explained, had issued many passes to citizens of Laon fleeing to Paris and the coast. But because now there were three German armies between Laon and Paris, the refugees had been turned back and their passes confiscated.

"From among them," said the officer, "we have selected one for you. It is issued to the wife of Count d'Aurillac, a captain of reserves, and her aunt, Madame Benet. It asks for those ladies and their chauffeur, Briand, a safe conduct through the French military lines. If it gets you into Paris you will destroy it and assume another name. The Count d'Aurillac is now with his regiment in that city. If he learned of the presence there of his wife, he would seek her, and that would not be good for you. So, if you reach Paris, you will become a Belgian refugee. You are high-born and rich. Your château has been destroyed. But you have money. You will give liberally to the Red Cross. You will volunteer to nurse in the hospitals. With your sad story of ill treatment by us, with your high birth, and your knowledge of nursing, which you acquired, of course, only as an amateur, you should not find it difficult to join the Ladies of France, or the American Ambulance. What you learn from the wounded English and French officers and the French doctors you will send us through the usual channels."

"When do I start?" asked the woman.

"For a few days," explained the officer, "you remain in this château. You will keep us informed of what is going forward after we withdraw."

"Withdraw?" It was more of an exclamation than a question. Marie was too well trained to ask questions.

"We are taking up a new position," said the officer, "on the Aisne."

The woman, incredulous, stared.

"And we do not enter Paris?"

"*You* do," returned the officer. "That is all that concerns you. We will join you later—in the spring. Meanwhile, for the winter we intrench ourselves along the Aisne. In a chimney of this château we have set up a wireless outfit. We are leaving it intact. The chauffeur Briand—who, you must explain to the French, you brought with you from Laon, and who has been long in your service —will transmit whatever you discover. We wish especially to know of any movement toward our left. If they attack in front from Soissons, we are prepared; but you must warn us of any attempt to cross the Oise and take us in flank."

The officer rose and hung upon himself his field glasses, map cases, and side arms.

"We leave you now," he said. "When the French arrive you will tell them your reason for halting at this château was that the owner, Monsieur Iverney, and his family are friends of your husband. You found us here, and we detained you. And so long as you can use the wireless, make excuses to remain. If they offer to send you on to

Paris, tell them your aunt is too ill to travel.''

"But they will find the wireless," said the woman. "They are sure to use the towers for observation, and they will find it."

"In that case," said the officer, "you will suggest to them that we fled in such haste we had no time to dismantle it. Of course, you had no knowledge that it existed, or, as a loyal French woman, you would have at once told them." To emphasize his next words the officer pointed at her: "Under no circumstances," he continued, "must you be suspected. If they should take Briand in the act, should they have even the least doubt concerning him, you must repudiate him entirely. If necessary, to keep your own skirts clear, it would be your duty yourself to denounce him as a spy."

"Your first orders," said the woman, "were to tell them Briand had been long in my service; that I brought him from my home in Laon."

"He might be in your service for years," returned the colonel, "and you not know he was a German agent."

"If to save myself I inform upon him," said Marie, "of course you know you will lose him."

The officer shrugged his shoulders. "A wireless operator," he retorted, "we can replace. But for you, and for the service you are to render in Paris, we have no substitute. *You* must not be found out. You are invaluable."

The spy inclined her head. "I thank you," she said.

The officer sputtered indignantly.

"It is not a compliment," he exclaimed; "it is

an order. You must not be found out!"

Withdrawn some two hundred yards from the Paris road, the château stood upon a wooded hill. Except directly in front, trees of great height surrounded it. The tips of their branches brushed the windows; interlacing, they continued until they overhung the wall of the estate. Where it ran with the road the wall gave way to a lofty gate and iron fence, through which those passing could see a stretch of noble turf, as wide as a polo field, borders of flowers disappearing under the shadows of the trees; and the château itself, with its terrace, its many windows, its high-pitched, sloping roof broken by towers and turrets.

Through the remainder of the night there came from the road to those in the château the roar and rumbling of the army in retreat. It moved without panic, disorder, or haste, but unceasingly. Not for an instant was there a breathing spell. And when the sun rose, the three spies—the two women and the chauffeur—who in the great château were now alone, could see as well as hear the gray column of steel rolling past below them.

The spies knew that the gray column had reached Claye, had stood within fifteen miles of Paris, and then had turned back. They knew also that the reverberations from the direction of Meaux, which each moment grew more loud and savage, were the French "seventy-fives" whipping the gray column forward. Of what they felt the Germans did not speak. In silence they looked at each other, and in the eyes of Marie was bitterness and resolve.

Toward noon Marie met Anfossi in the great drawing-room that stretched the length of the terrace and from the windows of which, through the park gates, they could see the Paris road.

"This, that is passing now," said Marie, "is the last of our rear guard. Go to your tower," she ordered, "and send word that except for stragglers and the wounded our column has just passed through Neufchelles, and that any moment we expect the French." She raised her hand impressively. "From now on," she warned, "we speak French, we think French, we *are* French!"

Anfossi, or Briand, as now he called himself, addressed her in that language. His tone was bitter. "Pardon my lese-majesty," he said, "but this chief of your Intelligence Department is a *dummer Mensch*. He is throwing away a valuable life."

Marie exclaimed in dismay. She placed her hand upon his arm, and the violet eyes filled with concern.

"Not yours!" she protested.

"Absolutely!" returned the Italian. "I can send nothing by this knapsack wireless that they will not learn from others; from airmen, Uhlans, the peasants in the fields. And certainly I will be caught. Dead I am dead, but alive and in Paris the opportunities are unending. From the French Legion Etranger I have my honorable discharge. I am an expert wireless operator and in their Signal Corps I can easily find a place. Imagine me, then, on the Eiffel Tower. From the air I snatch news from all of France, from the Channel, the North

Sea. You and I could work together, as in Rome. But here, between the lines, with a pass from a village *sous préfet*, it is ridiculous. I am not afraid to die. But to die because someone else is stupid, that is hard."

Marie clasped his hand in both of hers.

"You must not speak of death," she cried; "you know I must carry out my order, that I must force you to take this risk. And you know that thought of harm to you tortures me!"

Quickly the young man disengaged his hand. The woman exclaimed with anger.

"Why do you doubt me?" she cried.

Briand protested vehemently.

"I do not doubt you."

"My affection, then?"

The young man protested miserably. "You make it very hard, mademoiselle," he cried. "You are my superior officer, I am your servant."

The woman interrupted eagerly.

"Ah, you are jealous!" she cried. "Is that why you are so cruel? But when I *tell* you I love you, and only you, can you not *feel* it is the truth?"

The young man frowned unhappily.

"My duty, mademoiselle!" he stammered.

With an exclamation of anger Marie left him. As the door slammed behind her, the young man drew a deep breath. On his face was the expression of ineffable relief.

In the hall Marie met her elderly companion, Bertha, now her aunt, Madame Benet.

"I heard quarreling," Bertha protested. "It is most indiscreet."

Marie laughed noiselessly and drew her farther down the hall. "He is an imbecile!" she exclaimed. "He will kill me with his solemn face and his conceit."

Madame Benet frowned.

"He is a gentleman!"

"An Italian gentleman," returned Marie, "does not serve in the Belgian Congo unless it is the choice of that or the marble quarries."

"I do not know what his past may be," sighed Madame Benet, "nor do I ask. He is only a number, as you and I are only numbers. And I beg you to let us work in harmony."

Marie would have answered sharply, but on the instant her interest was diverted. For one week, by day and night, she had lived in a world peopled only by German soldiers. Beside her in the railroad carriage, on the station platforms, at the windows of the trains that passed the one in which she rode, at the grade crossings, on the bridges, in the roads that paralleled the tracks, choking the streets of the villages and spread over the fields of grain, she had seen only the gray-green uniforms. Even her professional eye no longer distinguished regiment from regiment, dragoon from grenadier, Uhlan from Hussar or Landsturm. Stripes, insignia, numerals, badges of rank, had lost their meaning. Those who wore them no longer were individuals. They were not even human. During the last three days the automobile, like a motorboat fighting the tide, had crept through a gray-green river of men stained, as though from the banks, by mud and yellow clay. And for hours, while the car was blocked, and in fury the engine raced and purred, the gray-green river had rolled past her, slowly but as inevitably as lava down the slope of a volcano, bearing on its surface faces with staring eyes, thousands and thousands of eyes, some fierce and bloodshot, others filled with weariness, homesickness, pain. At night she still saw them: the white faces under the sweat and dust, the eyes dumb, inarticulate, asking the answer. She had been suffocated by German soldiers, by the mass of them, engulfed and smothered; she had stifled in a land inhabited only by green-gray ghosts.

And suddenly, as though a miracle had been wrought, she saw upon the lawn, riding toward her, a man in scarlet, blue, and silver. One man riding alone.

Approaching with confidence, but alert, his reins fallen, his hands nursing his carbine, his eyes searched the shadows of the trees, the empty windows, even the sun-swept sky. His was the new face at the door, the new step on the floor. And the spy knew that had she beheld an army corps it would have been no more significant, no more menacing, than the solitary *chasseur à cheval* scouting in advance of the enemy.

"We are saved!" exclaimed Marie, with irony. "Go quickly," she commanded, "to the bedroom on the second floor that opens upon the staircase, so that you can see all who pass. You are too ill to travel. They must find you in bed."

"And you?" said Bertha.

"I," cried Marie rapturously, "hasten to welcome our preserver!"

The preserver was a peasant lad. Under the white dust his cheeks were burned a brown-red, his eyes, honest and blue, were puckered and encircled with tiny wrinkles through much staring at the skies and at horizon lines. Responsibility had made him older than his years, and in speech brief. He was unimpressed with the beautiful lady who with tears of joy ran to greet him, and who in an ecstasy of happiness pressed her cheek against the nose of his horse. He returned to her her papers and gravely echoed her answers to his questions. "This château," he repeated, "was occupied by their General Staff; they have left no wounded here; you saw the last of them pass a half-hour since." He gathered up his reins.

Marie shrieked in alarm. "You will not leave us?" she cried.

For the first time the young man permitted himself to smile. "Others arrive soon," he said.

He touched his shako, wheeled his horse in the direction from which he had come, and a minute later Marie heard the hoofs echoing through the empty village.

When they came, the others were more sympathetic. Even in times of war a beautiful woman is still a beautiful woman. And the staff officers who moved into the quarters so lately occupied by the enemy found in the presence of the Countess d'Aurillac nothing to distress them. In the absence of her dear friend, Madame Iverney, the châtelaine of the château, she acted as their hostess. Her chauffeur showed the company cooks the way to the kitchen, the larder, and the charcoal box. She herself placed the keys of the famous wine cellar in the hands of General André and intrusted those of the linen closet to the surgeon, that the wounded might be freshly bandaged. After the indignities she had suffered while "detained" by *les Boches*, her delight and relief at again finding herself under the protection of her own people would have touched a heart of stone. And the hearts of the staff were not of stone. It was with regret they gave the countess permission to continue on her way. At this she exclaimed with gratitude. She assured them that were her aunt able to travel she would immediately depart.

"In Paris she will be more comfortable than here," said the kind surgeon. He was a reservist, and in times of peace a fashionable physician and as much at his ease in a boudoir as in a field hospital. "Perhaps if I saw Madame Benet?"

At the suggestion the countess was overjoyed. But they found Madame Benet in a state of complete collapse. The conduct of the Germans had brought about a nervous breakdown.

"Though the bridges are destroyed at Meaux," urged the surgeon, "even with a detour you can be in Paris in four hours. I think it is worth the effort."

But the mere thought of the journey threw Madame Benet into hysterics. She asked only to rest, she begged for an opiate to make her sleep. She begged also that they would leave the door open, so that when she dreamed she was still in the hands of the Germans, and woke in terror, the sound of the dear French voices and the sight of the beloved French uniforms might reassure her. She played her part well. Marie felt not the least anxiety concerning her. But the new arrivals were less easily satisfied with Briand, the chauffeur.

The general sent his adjutant for the countess. When the adjutant had closed the door General André began abruptly:

"The chauffeur Briand," he asked, "you know him; you can vouch for him?"

"But, certainly!" protested Marie. "He is an Italian."

As though with sudden enlightenment, Marie laughed. It was as if now she saw a certain reasonableness in the suspicion of the officer. "Briand was so long in the Foreign Legion in Algiers," she explained, "where my husband found him, that we have come to think of him as French. As much French as ourselves, I assure you."

The general and his adjutant were regarding each other questioningly.

"Perhaps I should tell the countess," began the general, "that we have learned—"

The signal from the adjutant was so slight, so swift, that Marie barely intercepted it.

The lips of the general shut together like the leaves of a book. To show that the interview was at an end, he reached for a pen.

"I thank you," he said.

"Of course," prompted the adjutant, "Madame d'Aurillac understands the man must not know we inquired concerning him."

General André frowned at Marie.

"Certainly not!" he commanded. "The honest

fellow must not know that he was doubted even for a moment."

Marie raised the violet eyes reprovingly.

"I trust," she said with reproach, "I too well understand the feelings of a French soldier to let him know his loyalty is questioned."

With a murmur of appreciation the officers bowed and with a gesture of gracious pardon Marie left them.

Outside in the hall, with none but orderlies to observe, the graciousness fell from her like a cloak. She was drawn two ways. In her work Anfossi was valuable. But Anfossi suspected was less than of no value; he became a menace, a death warrant.

General André had said, "We have learned—" and the adjutant had halted him. What had he learned? Marie would have given much to know that. Still, one important fact comforted her. Anfossi alone was suspected. Had there been the slightest doubt concerning herself, they certainly would not have allowed her to guess her companion was under surveillance; they would not have asked one who was herself suspected to vouch for the innocence of a fellow conspirator. Marie found the course to follow difficult. With Anfossi under suspicion his usefulness was for the moment at an end; and to accept the chance offered her to continue on to Paris seemed most wise. On the other hand, if she had succeeded in allaying their doubts concerning Anfossi, the results most to be desired could be attained only by remaining where they were.

Their position inside the lines was of the greatest strategic value. The rooms of the servants were under the roof, and that Briand should sleep in one of them was natural. That to reach or leave his room he should constantly be ascending or descending the stairs also was natural. The field-wireless outfit, or, as he had disdainfully described it, the "knapsack" wireless, was situated not in the bedroom he had selected for himself, but in one adjoining. At other times this was occupied by the maid of Madame Iverney. To summon her maid Madame Iverney had but to press a button from her apartment on the second floor. And it was in the apartment of Madame Iverney, and on the bed of that lady, that Madame Benet now reclined. When through the open door she saw an officer or soldier mount the stairs, she pressed the button that rang a bell in the room of the maid. In this way, long before whoever was ascending the stairs could reach the top floor, warning of his approach came to Anfossi. It gave him time to replace the dustboard over the fireplace in which the wireless was concealed and to escape into his own bedroom. The arrangement was ideal. And already information picked up in the halls below by Marie had been conveyed to Anfossi to relay in a French cipher to the German General Staff at Rheims.

Marie made an alert and charming hostess. To all who saw her it was evident that her mind was intent only upon the comfort of her guests. Throughout the day many came and went, but she made each welcome; to each as he departed she called *"bonne chance."* Efficient, tireless, tactful, she was everywhere: in the dining room, in the kitchen, in the bedrooms, finding mattresses to spread for the wounded in the gorgeous salons of the champagne prince; carrying wine into the courtyard for the soldier-chauffeurs. At all times an alluring person, now the one woman in a tumult of men, her smart frock covered by an apron, her head and arms bare, undismayed by the sight of the wounded or by the distant rumble of the guns, the Countess d'Aurillac was an inspiring and beautiful picture. The eyes of the officers, young and old, informed her of that fact. By the morning of the next day she was accepted as the owner of the château. And though she continually reminded the staff she was present only as the friend of her schoolmate, Madame Iverney, they deferred to her as to a hostess. Many of them she already saluted by name, and she was particularly kind to those who were constantly motoring to and from the front at Soissons with messages. Overnight the legend of her charm, of her devotion to the soldiers of all ranks, had spread from Soissons to Meaux, and from Meaux to Paris.

It was noon of that day when from the window of the second story Marie saw an armored automobile sweep into the courtyard. It was driven by an officer, young and appallingly good-looking, and, as was obvious by the way he spun his car, one who held in contempt both the law of gravity and death. That he was someone of importance seemed evident. Before he could alight, the adjutant had raced to meet him. With her eye for detail Marie observed that the young officer, instead of imparting information, received it. He must, she guessed, have just arrived from Paris, and his brother officer either was telling him the news or giving him his orders. Whichever it might be, the new arrival was greatly interested in what was told him. One instant his gauntleted fist beat upon the steering wheel in indignation, the next he smiled with pleasure. To interpret this pantomime was difficult; and, the better to inform herself, Marie descended the stairs.

As she reached the lower hall the two officers entered. To the spy the last man to arrive was always the one of greatest importance; and Marie assured herself that through her friend, the adjutant, meeting with this one would prove easy.

But the chauffeur-commander of the armored car made it most difficult. At sight of Marie, he snatched his kepi from his head and sprang toward her, as though greeting a dear friend.

"The major," he cried, "told me you were here, that you are Madame d'Aurillac." His eyes spoke his admiration. In delight he beamed upon her. "I might have known it!" he murmured. With the confidence of one who is sure he brings good news, he laughed happily. "And I," he cried, "am 'Pierrot'!"

Who the devil "Pierrot" might be the spy could not guess. She knew only that she wished "Pierrot" and his car had been blown to tiny fragments by a German shell. Was it a trap, she asked herself, or was the handsome youth really someone the

Countess d'Aurillac should know. But, since from introducing himself it was evident he could not know that lady very well, Marie took courage and smiled.

"Which 'Pierrot'?" she parried.

"Pierre Thierry!" cried the youth.

To Marie's relief he turned upon the adjutant and explained who Pierre Thierry might be.

"Paul d'Aurillac," he said, "is my dearest friend. When he married this charming lady I was stationed in Algiers, and but for the war I might never have met her."

He bowed to Marie, with his hand on his heart in a most charming manner. He made no effort to conceal his admiration.

"And so," he said, "I know why there is war!"

The adjutant smiled indulgently and departed on his duties, leaving them alone. The handsome eyes of Captain Thierry were raised to the violet eyes of Marie. They appraised her boldly and as boldly expressed their approval.

In burlesque the young man exclaimed indignantly: "Paul deceived me!" he cried. "He told me he had married the most beautiful woman in Laon. He has married the most beautiful woman in France!"

To Marie this was not impertinence, but gallantry.

This was a language she understood, and this was the type of man she held most in contempt, because he was the least difficult to manage.

"But about you, Paul did not deceive me," she

retorted. In apparent confusion her eyes refused to meet his. "He told me 'Pierrot' was a most dangerous man!"

She continued hurriedly. With wifely solicitude she asked concerning Paul. She explained that for a week she had been a prisoner in the château, and, since the mobilization, she had heard nothing of her husband save that he was with his regiment in Paris. Captain Thierry was able to give her later news. Only the day previous, on the boulevards, he had met Count d'Aurillac. He was at the Grand Hôtel, and as Thierry was at once motoring back to Paris he would give Paul news of their meeting. He hoped he might tell him that soon his wife also would be in Paris. Marie explained that only the illness of her aunt prevented her from joining her husband that same day. Her manner became serious.

"And what other news have you?" she asked. "Here on the firing line we know less of what is going forward than you in Paris."

So Pierre Thierry told her all he knew. They were preparing dispatches he was at once to carry back to the General Staff, and, for the moment, his time was his own. How could he better employ it than in talking of the war with a patriotic and charming French woman?

In consequence Marie acquired a mass of facts, gossip, and guesses. From these she mentally selected such information as would be of vital interest to her employers across the Aisne.

And now her only wish was to rid herself of Thierry and seek Anfossi on the fourth floor. But, in attempting this, she was delayed by the return of the adjutant. The adjutant gave Thierry a sealed envelope.

"Thirty-one, Boulevard des Invalides," he said. With a smile he turned to Marie. "And you will accompany him!"

"I!" exclaimed Marie. She was sick with sudden terror.

But the tolerant smile of the adjutant reassured her.

"The count, your husband," he explained, "has learned of your detention here by the enemy, and he has besieged the General Staff to have you convoyed safely to Paris." The adjutant glanced at a field telegram he held open in his hand. "He asks," he continued, "that you be permitted to return in the car of his friend, Captain Thierry, and that on arriving you join him at the Grand Hôtel."

Thierry exclaimed with delight.

"But how charming!" he cried. "Tonight you must both dine with me at La Rue's." He saluted his superior officer. "Some petrol, sir," he said, "and I am ready." To Marie he added: "The car will be at the steps in five minutes." He turned and left them.

The thoughts of Marie, snatching at an excuse for delay, raced madly. The danger of meeting the Count d'Aurillac, her supposed husband, did not alarm her. The Grand Hôtel has many exits, and even before they reached it, she could invent an excuse for leaving the car that the gallant Thierry would not suspect. But what now concerned her

was how, before she was whisked away to Paris,
she could convey to Anfossi the information she
had gathered from Thierry. First, she gave an
excellent imitation of a woman overcome with
delight at being reunited with her husband. Then
she exclaimed in distress: "But my aunt, Madame
Benet!" she cried. "I cannot leave her!"

"The Sisters of St. Francis," said the adjutant,
"arrive within an hour to nurse the wounded.
They will care also for your aunt."

Marie concealed her chagrin. "Then I will prepare to go at once," she said.

The adjutant handed her a slip of paper. "Your
laisser-passer to Paris," he said. "You leave in five
minutes, madame!"

As temporary hostess of the château Marie was
free to visit any part of it, and as she passed her
door a signal from Madame Benet told her that
Anfossi was on the fourth floor, that he was at
work, and that the coast was clear. Softly, in the
felt slippers she always wore, as she explained, in
order not to disturb the wounded, she mounted
the staircase. In her hand she carried the house-
keeper's keys, and as an excuse it was her plan to
return with an armful of linen for the arriving
Sisters. But Marie never reached the top of the
stairs. When her eyes rose to the level of the
fourth floor she came to a sudden halt. At what
she saw terror gripped her, bound her hand and
foot, and turned her blood to ice.

At her post Madame Benet had slept, for an
instant, and an officer of the staff, led by curiosity,
chance, or suspicion, had, unobserved and unan-

nounced, mounted to the fourth floor. When Marie saw him he was in front of the room that held the wireless. His back was toward her, but she saw that he was holding the door to the room ajar, that his eye was pressed to the opening, and that through it he had pushed the muzzle of his automatic. Marie knew what would be the fate of Anfossi. Nor did she for an instant consider it. Her thoughts were of her own safety; that she might live. Not that she might still serve the Wilhelmstrasse, the Kaiser, or the Fatherland; but that she might live. In a moment Anfossi would be denounced, the château would ring with the alarm, and, though she knew Anfossi would not betray her, she might be accused by others. To avert suspicion from herself she saw only one way open. She must be the first to denounce Anfossi.

Like a deer she leaped down the marble stairs and, in a panic she had no need to assume, burst into the presence of the staff.

"Gentlemen!" she gasped. "My servant—the chauffeur—Briand is a spy! There is a German wireless in the château. He is using it! I have seen him." With exclamations, the officers rose to their feet. General André alone remained seated. General André was a veteran of many Colonial wars: Cochin-China, Algiers, Morocco. The great war, when it came, found him on duty in the Intelligence Department. His aquiline nose, bristling white eyebrows, and flashing, restless eyes gave him his nickname of *l'Aigle*.

In amazement, the flashing eyes were now turned upon Marie. He glared at her as though he thought she had suddenly gone mad.

"A German wireless!" he protested. "It is impossible!"

"I was on the fourth floor," panted Marie, "collecting linen for the Sisters. In the room next to the linen closet I heard a strange buzzing sound. I opened the door softly. I saw Briand with his back to me seated by an instrument. There were receivers clamped to his ears! My God! The disgrace. The disgrace to my husband and to me, who vouched for him to you!" Apparently in an agony of remorse, the fingers of the woman laced and interlaced. "I cannot forgive myself!"

The officers moved toward the door, but General André halted them. Still in a tone of incredulity, he demanded: "When did you see this?"

Marie knew the question was coming, knew she must explain how she saw Briand and yet did not see the staff officer who, with his prisoner, might appear at any instant. She must make it plain she had discovered the spy and left the upper part of the house before the officer had visited it. When that was she could not know, but the chance was that he had preceded her by only a few minutes.

"When did you see this?" repeated the general.

"But just now," cried Marie; "not ten minutes since."

"Why did you not come to me at once?"

"I was afraid," replied Marie. "If I moved I was afraid he might hear me, and he, knowing I would expose him, would kill me—and so *escape you!*" There was an eager whisper of approval. For silence, General André slapped his hand upon the table.

"Then," continued Marie, "I realized that with the receivers on his ears he could not have heard me open the door, nor could he hear me leave, and I ran to my aunt. The thought that we had harbored such an animal sickened me, and I was weak enough to feel faint. But only for an instant. Then I came here." She moved swiftly to the door. "Let me show you the room," she begged; "you can take him in the act." Her eyes, wild with the excitement of the chase, swept the circle. "Will you come?" she begged.

Unconscious of the crisis he interrupted, the orderly on duty opened the door.

"Captain Thierry's compliments," he recited mechanically, "and is he to delay longer for Madame d'Aurillac?"

With a sharp gesture General André waved Marie toward the door. Without rising, he inclined his head. "Adieu, madame," he said. "We act at once upon your information. I thank you!"

As she crossed from the hall to the terrace, the ears of the spy were assaulted by a sudden tumult of voices. They were raised in threats and curses. Looking back, she saw Anfossi descending the stairs. His hands were held above his head; behind him, with his automatic, the staff officer she had surprised on the fourth floor was driving him forward. Above the clenched fists of the soldiers that ran to meet him, the eyes of Anfossi were turned toward her. His face was expressionless.

His eyes neither accused nor reproached. And with the joy of one who has looked upon and then escaped the guillotine, Marie ran down the steps to the waiting automobile. With a pretty cry of pleasure she leaped into the seat beside Thierry. Gayly she threw out her arms. "To Paris!" she commanded. The handsome eyes of Thierry, eloquent with admiration, looked back into hers. He stooped, threw in the clutch, and the great gray car, with the machine gun and its crew of privates guarding the rear, plunged through the park.

"To Paris!" echoed Thierry.

In the order in which Marie had last seen them, Anfossi and the staff officer entered the room of General André, and the door was shut. The face of the staff officer was grave, but his voice could not conceal his elation.

"My general," he reported, "I found this man in the act of giving information to the enemy. There is a wireless—"

General André rose slowly. He looked neither at the officer nor at his prisoner. With frowning eyes he stared down at the maps upon his table.

"I know," he interrupted. "Someone has already told me." He paused, and then, as though recalling his manners, but still without raising his eyes, he added: "You have done well, sir."

In silence the staff officers stood motionless. With surprise they noted that, as yet, neither in anger nor curiosity had General André glanced at the prisoner. But the spy was most acutely conscious of the presence of the general. He stood erect, his arms still raised, but his body strained forward, and his own eyes were fixed on the averted eyes of the general.

In an agony of supplication they asked a question.

At last, as though against his wish, the general turned his head toward the spy, and their eyes met. And still General André was silent. Then the arms of the spy fell to his sides, like those of a runner who has finished his race and breasts the tape exhausted. In a voice low and vibrant he spoke his question.

"It has been so long, sir," he pleaded. "May I not come home?"

General André turned to the astonished group surrounding him. His voice was hushed like that of one who speaks across an open grave.

"Gentlemen," he began, "my children," he added. "A German spy, a woman, involved your brother in arms, Henri Ravignac, in a scandal. His honor, he thought, was concerned, and he refused to live without honor. To prove him guiltless his younger brother Charles asked leave to seek out the woman who had betrayed Henri, and was detailed by us on secret service. He gave up home, family, friends. He lived in exile, in poverty, at all times in danger of a swift and ignoble death. In the War Office we know him as one who has given to his country services she cannot hope to reward. For she cannot return to him the years he has lost. She cannot return to him his brother. But she can and will clear the name of Henri Ravignac, and bestow upon his brother Charles promotion and honors."

The general turned and embraced the spy. "My children," he said, "welcome your brother. He has come home."

Before the car had reached the fortifications, Marie Gessler had arranged her plan of escape. She had departed from the château without even a handbag, and she would say that before the shops closed she must make purchases.

Le Printemps lay in their way, and she asked if when they reached it she might alight for a moment. Captain Thierry readily gave permission.

From the department store it would be most easy to disappear, and Marie smiled covertly in anticipation. Nor was the picture of Captain Thierry impatiently waiting outside unamusing.

But before Le Printemps was approached, the car turned sharply down a narrow street. On one side, along its entire length, ran a high gray wall, grim and forbidding. In it was a green gate studded with iron bolts. The automobile drew suddenly to a halt. The crew of the armored car tumbled off the rear seat, and one of them beat upon the green gate. Marie felt a hand of ice clutch at her throat. But she controlled herself.

"And what is this?" she cried gayly.

At her side Captain Thierry was smiling down at her, but his smile was hateful.

"It is the prison of St. Lazare," he said. "It is not becoming," he added sternly, "that the name of the Countess d'Aurillac should be made as common as the Paris road!"

Fighting for her life, Marie thrust herself against

him. The arm that throughout the journey she had rested on the back of the driving seat caressed his shoulders; her lips and the violet eyes were close to his.

"Why should you care?" she whispered fiercely. "You have *me*! Let the Count d'Aurillac look after the honor of his wife himself."

The charming Thierry laughed at her mockingly.

"He means to," he said. "I *am* the Count d'Aurillac!"

The Traitor

W. Somerset Maugham

When Ashenden, given charge of a number of spies working from Switzerland, was first sent there, R., wishing him to see the sort of reports that he would be required to obtain, handed him the communications, a sheaf of typewritten documents, of a man known in the secret service as Gustav.

"He's the best fellow we've got," said R. "His information is always very full and circumstantial. I want you to give his reports your very best attention. Of course Gustav is a clever little chap, but there's no reason why we shouldn't get just as good reports from the other agents. It's merely a question of explaining exactly what we want."

Gustav, who lived at Basle, represented a Swiss firm with branches at Frankfort, Mannheim and Cologne, and by virtue of his business was able to go in and out of Germany without risk. He traveled up and down the Rhine, and gathered material about the movement of troops, the manufacture of munitions, the state of mind of the country (a

point on which R. laid stress) and other matters
upon which the Allies desired information. His
frequent letters to his wife hid an ingenious code
and the moment she received them in Basle she
sent them to Ashenden in Geneva, who extracted
from them the important facts and communicated
these in the proper quarter. Every two months
Gustav came home and prepared one of the reports that served as models to the other spies in
this particular section of the secret service.

His employers were pleased with Gustav and
Gustav had reason to be pleased with his employers. His services were so useful that he was not
only paid more highly than the others but for
particular scoops had received from time to time a
handsome bonus.

This went on for more than a year. Then something aroused R.'s quick suspicions: he was a man
of an amazing alertness, not so much of mind, as
of instinct, and he had suddenly a feeling that
some hanky-panky was going on. He said nothing
definite to Ashenden (whatever R. surmised he
was disposed to keep to himself) but told him to go
to Basle, Gustav being then in Germany, and have
a talk with Gustav's wife. He left it to Ashenden
to decide the tenor of the conversation.

Having arrived at Basle, and leaving his bag at
the station, for he did not yet know whether he
would have to stay or not, he took a tram to the
corner of the street in which Gustav lived, and
with a quick look to see that he was not followed,
walked along to the house he sought. It was a
block of flats that gave you the impression of

decent poverty and Ashenden conjectured that they were inhabited by clerks and small trades-people. Just inside the door was a cobbler's shop and Ashenden stopped.

"Does Herr Grabow live here?" he asked in his none too fluent German.

"Yes, I saw him go up a few minutes ago. You'll find him in."

Ashenden was startled, for he had but the day before received through Gustav's wife a letter addressed from Mannheim in which Gustav by means of his code gave the numbers of certain regiments that had just crossed the Rhine. Ashenden thought it unwise to ask the cobbler the question that rose to his lips, so thanked him and went up to the third floor on which he knew already that Gustav lived. He rang the bell and heard it tinkle within. In a moment the door was opened by a dapper little man with a close-shaven round head and spectacles. He wore carpet slippers.

"Herr Grabow?" asked Ashenden.

"At your service," said Gustav.

"May I come in?"

Gustav was standing with his back to the light and Ashenden could not see the look on his face. He felt a momentary hesitation and gave the name under which he received Gustav's letters from Germany.

"Come in, come in. I am very glad to see you."

Gustav led the way into a stuffy little room, heavy with carved oak furniture, and on the large table covered with a tablecloth of green velveteen was a typewriter. Gustav was apparently engaged in composing one of his invaluable reports. A woman was sitting at the open window darning socks, but at a word from Gustav she rose, gathered up her things and left. Ashenden had disturbed a pretty picture of connubial bliss.

"Sit down, please. How very fortunate that I was in Basle! I have long wanted to make your acquaintance. I have only just this minute returned from Germany." He pointed to the sheets of paper by the typewriter. "I think you will be pleased with the news I bring. I have some very valuable information." He chuckled. "One is never sorry to earn a bonus."

He was very cordial, but to Ashenden his cordiality rang false. Gustav kept his eyes, smiling behind the glasses, fixed watchfully on Ashenden and it was possible that they held a trace of nervousness.

"You must have traveled quickly to get here only a few hours after your letter, sent here and then sent on by your wife, reached me in Geneva."

"That is very probable. One of the things I had to tell you is that the Germans suspect that information is getting through by means of commercial letters and so they have decided to hold up all mail at the frontier for eight and forty hours."

"I see," said Ashenden amiably. "And was it on that account that you took the precaution of dating your letter forty-eight hours after you sent it?"

"Did I do that? That was very stupid of me. I must have mistaken the day of the month."

Ashenden looked at Gustav with a smile. That was very thin; Gustav, a business man, knew too well how important in his particular job was the exactness of a date. The circuitous routes by which it was necessary to get information from Germany made it difficult to transmit news quickly and it was essential to know precisely on what days certain events had taken place.

"Let me look at your passport a minute," said Ashenden.

"What do you want with my passport?"

"I want to see when you went into Germany and when you came out."

"But you do not imagine that my comings and goings are marked on my passport? I have methods of crossing the frontier."

Ashenden knew a good deal of this matter. He knew that both the Germans and the Swiss guarded the frontier with severity.

"Oh? Why should you not cross in the ordinary way? You were engaged because your connection with a Swiss firm supplying necessary goods to Germany made it easy for you to travel backwards and forwards without suspicion. I can understand that you might get past the German sentries with the connivance of the Germans, but what about the Swiss?"

Gustav assumed a look of indignation.

"I do not understand you. Do you mean to suggest that I am in the service of the Germans? I give you my word of honor . . . I will not allow my straightforwardness to be impugned."

"You would not be the only one to take money from both sides and provide information of value to neither."

"Do you pretend that my information is of no value? Why then have you given me more bonuses than any other agent has received? The Colonel has repeatedly expressed the highest satisfaction with my services."

It was Ashenden's turn now to be cordial.

"Come, come, my dear fellow, do not try to ride the high horse. You do not wish to show me your passport and I will not insist. You are not under the impression that we leave the statements of our agents without corroboration or that we are so foolish as not to keep track of their movements? Even the best of jokes cannot bear an indefinite repetition. I am in peace time a humorist by profession and I tell you that from bitter experience." Now Ashenden thought the moment had arrived to attempt his bluff; he knew something of the excellent but difficult game of poker. "We have information that you have not been to Germany now, nor since you were engaged by us, but have sat here quietly in Basle, and all your reports are merely due to your fertile imagination."

Gustav looked at Ashenden and saw a face expressive of nothing but tolerance and good humor. A smile slowly broke on his lips and he gave his shoulders a little shrug.

"Did you think I was such a fool as to risk my life for fifty pounds a month? I love my wife."

Ashenden laughed outright.

"I congratulate you. It is not everyone who can flatter himself that he has made a fool of our secret service for a year."

"I had the chance of earning money without any difficulty. My firm stopped sending me into Germany at the beginning of the war, but I learned what I could from the other travelers, I kept my ears open in restaurants and beer cellars and I read the German papers. I got a lot of amusement out of sending you reports and letters."

"I don't wonder," said Ashenden.

"What are you going to do?"

"Nothing. What can we do? You are not under the impression that we shall continue to pay you a salary?"

"No, I cannot expect that."

"By the way, if it is not indiscreet, may I ask if you have been playing the same game with the Germans?"

"Oh, no," Gustav cried vehemently. "How can you think it? My sympathies are absolutely pro-Ally. My heart is entirely with you."

"Well, why not?" asked Ashenden. "The Germans have all the money in the world and there is no reason why you should not get some of it. We could give you information from time to time that the Germans would be prepared to pay for."

Gustav drummed his fingers on the table. He took up a sheet of the now useless report.

"The Germans are dangerous people to meddle with."

"You are a very intelligent man. And after all, even if your salary is stopped, you can always earn a bonus by bringing us news that can be useful to us. But it will have to be substantiated; in future we pay only by results."

"I will think of it."

For a moment or two Ashenden left Gustav to his reflections. He lit a cigarette and watched the smoke he had inhaled fade into the air. He thought too.

"Is there anything particular you want to know?" asked Gustav suddenly.

Ashenden smiled.

"It would be worth a couple of thousand Swiss francs to you if you could tell me what the Germans are doing with a spy of theirs in Lucerne. He is an Englishman and his name is Grantley Caypor."

"I have heard the name," said Gustav. He paused a moment. "How long are you staying here?"

"As long as necessary. I will take a room at the hotel and let you know the number. If you have anything to say to me you can be sure of finding me in my room at nine every morning and at seven every night."

"I should not risk coming to the hotel. But I can write."

"Very well."

Ashenden rose to go and Gustav accompanied him to the door.

"We part without ill-feeling then?" he asked.

"Of course. Your reports will remain in our archives as models of what a report should be."

Ashenden spent two or three days visiting Basle.

It did not much amuse him. He passed a good deal of time in the bookshops turning over the pages of books that would have been worth reading if life were a thousand years long. Once he saw Gustav in the street. On the fourth morning a letter was brought up with his coffee. The envelope was that of a commercial firm unknown to him and inside it was a typewritten sheet. There was no address and no signature. Ashenden wondered if Gustav was aware that a typewriter could betray its owner as certainly as handwriting. Having twice carefully read the letter, he held the paper up to the light to see the watermark (he had no reason for doing this except that the sleuths of detective novels always did it), then struck a match and watched it burn. He scrunched up the charred fragments in his hand.

He got up, for he had taken advantage of his situation to breakfast in bed, packed his bag and took the next train to Berne. From there he was able to send a code telegram to R. His instructions were given to him verbally two days later, in the bedroom of his hotel at an hour when no one was likely to be seen walking along a corridor, and within twenty-four hours, though by a circuitous route, he arrived at Lucerne.

Having taken a room at the hotel at which he had been instructed to stay, Ashenden went out; it was a lovely day, early in August, and the sun shone in an unclouded sky. He had not been to Lucerne since he was a boy and but vaguely remembered a covered bridge, a great stone lion and a church in which he had sat, bored yet impressed, while they played an organ; and now wandering along a shady quay (and the lake looked just as tawdry and unreal as it looked on the picture-postcards) he tried not so much to find his way about a half-forgotten scene as to reform in his mind some recollection of the shy and eager lad, so impatient for life (which he saw not in the present of his adolescence but only in the future of his manhood), who so long ago had wandered there. But it seemed to him that the most vivid of his memories was not of himself, but of the crowd; he seemed to remember sun and heat and people; the train was crowded and so was the hotel, the lake streamers were packed and on the quays and in the streets you threaded your way among the throng of holiday makers. They were fat and old and ugly and odd, and they stank.

Now, in wartime, Lucerne was as deserted as it must have been before the world at large discovered that Switzerland was the playground of Europe. Most of the hotels were closed, the streets were empty, the rowing boats for hire rocked idly at the water's edge and there was none to take them, and in the avenues by the lake the only persons to be seen were serious Swiss taking their neutrality, like a dachshund, for a walk with them. Ashenden felt exhilarated by the solitude, and sitting down on a bench that faced the water surrendered himself deliberately to the sensation. It was true that the lake was absurd, the water was too blue, the mountains too snowy, and its beauty, hitting you in the face, exasperated rather than thrilled; but all the same there was something pleasing in the prospect, an artless candor, like one of Mendelssohn's *Songs Without Words,* that made Ashenden smile with complacency. Lucerne reminded him of wax flowers under glass cases and cuckoo clocks and fancy work in Berlin wool. So long at all events as the fine weather lasted he was prepared to enjoy himself. He did not see why he should not at least try to combine pleasure to himself with profit to his country. He was traveling with a brand-new passport in his pocket, under a borrowed name, and this gave him an agreeable sense of owning a new personality. He was often slightly tired of himself, and it diverted him for a while to be merely a creature of R.'s facile invention. The experience he had just enjoyed appealed to his acute sense of the absurd. R., it is true, had not seen the fun of it: what humor R. possessed was of a sardonic turn and he had no facility for taking in good part a joke at his own expense. To do that you must be able to look at yourself from the outside and be at the same time spectator and actor in the pleasant comedy of life. R. was a soldier and regarded introspection as unhealthy, un-English and unpatriotic.

Ashenden got up and strolled slowly to his hotel. It was a small German hotel, of the second class, spotlessly clean, and his bedroom had a nice view; it was furnished with brightly varnished pitch-pine, and though on a cold wet day it would have been wretched, in that warm and sunny weather it was gay and pleasing. There were tables in the hall and he sat down at one of these and ordered a bottle of beer. The landlady was curious to know why in that dead season he had come to stay and he was glad to satisfy her curiosity. He told her that he had recently recovered from an attack of typhoid and had come to Lucerne to get back his strength. He was employed in the Censorship Department and was taking the opportunity to brush up his rusty German. He asked her if she could recommend to him a German teacher. The landlady was a blond and blowsy Swiss, good-humored and talkative, so that Ashenden felt pretty sure that she would repeat in the proper quarter the information he gave her. It was his turn now to ask a few questions. She was voluble on the subject of the war on account of which the hotel, in that month so full that rooms had to be found for visitors in neighboring houses, was nearly empty. A few people came in from outside to eat their meals *en pension*, but she had only two lots of resident guests. One was an old Irish couple who lived in Vevey and passed their summers in Lucerne and the other was an Englishman and his wife. She was a German and they were obliged on that account to live in a neutral country. Ashenden took care to show little curiosity about them—he recognized in the description Grantley Caypor—but of her own accord she told him that they spent most of the day walking about the mountains. Herr Caypor was a botanist and much interested in the flora of the country. His lady was a very nice woman and she felt her position keenly. Ah, well, the war could not last forever. The landlady bustled away and Ashenden went upstairs.

Dinner was at seven, and, wishing to be in the dining room before anyone else so that he could take stock of his fellow-guests as they entered, he went down as soon as he heard the bell. It was a very plain, stiff, whitewashed room, with chairs of the same shiny pitch-pine as in his bedroom, and on the walls were oleographs of Swiss lakes. On each little table was a bunch of flowers. It was all neat and clean and presaged a bad dinner. Ashenden would have liked to make up for it by ordering a bottle of the best Rhine wine to be found in the hotel, but did not venture to draw attention to himself by extravagance (he saw on two or three tables half-empty bottles of table hock, which made him surmise that his fellow-guests drank thriftily), and so contented himself with ordering a pint of lager. Presently one or two persons came in, single men with some occupation in Lucerne and obviously Swiss, and sat down each at his own little table and untied the napkins that at the end of luncheon they had neatly tied up. They propped newspapers against their water jugs and read while they somewhat noisily ate their soup. Then entered a very old tall bent man, with white hair and a drooping white moustache, accompanied by a little old white-haired lady in black. These were certainly the Irish colonel and his wife of whom the landlady had spoken. They took their seats and the colonel poured out a thimbleful of wine for his wife and a thimbleful for himself. They waited in silence for their dinner to be served to them by the buxom, hearty maid.

At last the persons arrived for whom Ashenden

had been waiting. He was doing his best to read a German book and it was only by an exercise of self-control that he allowed himself only for one instant to raise his eyes as they came in. His glance showed him a man of about forty-five with short dark hair, somewhat grizzled, of middle height, but corpulent, with a broad red clean-shaven face. He wore a shirt open at the neck, with a wide collar, and a gray suit. He walked ahead of his wife, and of her Ashenden only caught the impression of a German woman self-effaced and dusty. Grantley Caypor sat down and began in a loud voice explaining to the waitress that they had taken an immense walk. They had been up some mountain the name of which meant nothing to Ashenden but which excited in the maid expressions of astonishment and enthusiasm. Then Caypor, still in fluent German but with a marked English accent, said that they were so late they had not even gone up to wash, but had just rinsed their hands outside. He had a resonant voice and a jovial manner.

"Serve me quick, we're starving with hunger, and bring beer, bring three bottles. *Lieber Gott*, what a thirst I have!"

He seemed to be a man of exuberant vitality. He brought into that dull, overclean dining room the breath of life and everyone in it appeared of a sudden more alert. He began to talk to his wife, in English, and everything he said could be heard by all; but presently she interrupted him with a remark made in an undertone. Caypor stopped and Ashenden felt that his eyes were turned in his direction. Mrs. Caypor had noticed the arrival of a stranger and had drawn her husband's attention to it. Ashenden turned the page of the book he was pretending to read, but he felt that Caypor's gaze was fixed intently upon him. When he addressed his wife again it was in so low a tone that Ashenden could not even tell what language he used, but when the maid brought them their soup Caypor, his voice still low, asked her a question. It was plain that he was inquiring who Ashenden was. Ashenden could catch of the maid's reply but the one word *länder*.

One or two people finished their dinner and went out picking their teeth. The old Irish colonel and his old wife rose from their table and he stood aside to let her pass. They had eaten their meal without exchanging a word. She walked slowly to the door; but the colonel stopped to say a word to a Swiss who might have been a local attorney, and when she reached it she stood there, bowed and with a sheeplike look, patiently waiting for her husband to come and open it for her. Ashenden realized that she had never opened a door for herself. She did not know how to. In a minute the colonel with his old, old gait came to the door and opened it; she passed out and he followed. The little incident offered a key to their whole lives, and from it Ashenden began to reconstruct their histories, circumstances and characters; but he pulled himself up: he could not allow himself the luxury of creation. He finished his dinner.

When he went into the hall he saw tied to the leg of a table a bull terrier and in passing mechani-

cally put down his hand to fondle the dog's drooping, soft ears. The landlady was standing at the
foot of the stairs.

"Whose is this lovely beast?" asked Ashenden.

"He belongs to Herr Caypor. Fritzi, he is called.
Herr Caypor says he has a longer pedigree than the
King of England."

Fritzi rubbed himself against Ashenden's leg
and with his nose sought the palm of his hand.
Ashenden went upstairs to fetch his hat, and
when he came down saw Caypor standing at the
entrance of the hotel talking with the landlady.
From the sudden silence and their constrained
manner he guessed that Caypor had been making
inquiries about him. When he passed between
them, into the street, out of the corner of his eye
he saw Caypor give him a suspicious stare. That
frank, jovial red face bore then a look of shifty
cunning.

Ashenden strolled along till he found a tavern
where he could have his coffee in the open. He was
pleased at last to have come face to face with the
man of whom he had heard so much and in a day
or two hoped to become acquainted with him. It is
never very difficult to get to know anyone who has
a dog. But he was in no hurry; he would let things
take their course: with the object he had in view
he could not afford to be hasty.

Ashenden reviewed the circumstances.
Grantley Caypor was an Englishman, born according to his passport in Birmingham, and he was
forty-two years of age. His wife, to whom he had
been married for eleven years, was of Germa-

birth and parentage. That was public knowledge. Information about his antecedents was contained in a private document. He had started life, according to this, in a lawyer's office in Birmingham and then had drifted into journalism. He had been connected with an English paper in Cairo and with another in Shanghai. There he got into trouble for attempting to get money on false pretenses and was sentenced to a short term of imprisonment. All trace of him was lost for two years after his release, when he reappeared in a shipping office in Marseilles. From there, still in the shipping business, he went to Hamburg, where he married, and to London. In London he set up for himself, in the export business, but after some time failed and was made a bankrupt. He returned to journalism. At the outbreak of war he was once more in the shipping business and in August 1914 was living quietly with his German wife at Southampton. In the beginning of the following year he told his employers that owing to the nationality of his wife his position was intolerable; they had no fault to find with him and, recognizing that he was in an awkward fix, granted his request that he should be transferred to Genoa. Here he remained till Italy entered the war, but then gave notice and with his papers in perfect order crossed the border and took up his residence in Switzerland.

All this indicated a man of doubtful honesty and unsettled disposition, with no background and of no financial standing; but the facts were of no importance to anyone till it was discovered that

Caypor, certainly from the beginning of the war and perhaps sooner, was in the service of the German Intelligence Department. He had a salary of forty pounds a month. But though dangerous and wily, no steps would have been taken to deal with him if he had contented himself with transmitting such news as he was able to gain in Switzerland. He could do no great harm there and it might even be possible to make use of him to convey information that it was desirable to let the enemy have. He had no notion that anything was known of him. His letters, and he received a good many, were closely censored; there were few codes that the people who dealt with such matters could not in the end decipher and it might be that sooner or later through him it would be possible to lay hands on the organization that still flourished in England. But then he did something that drew R.'s attention to him. Had he known it, none could have blamed him for shaking in his shoes: R. was not a very nice man to get on the wrong side of. Caypor scraped acquaintance in Zürich with a young Spaniard, Gomez by name, who had lately entered the British secret service, by his nationality inspired him with confidence, and managed to worm out of him the fact that he was engaged in espionage. Probably the Spaniard, with a very human desire to seem important, had done no more than talk mysteriously; but on Caypor's information he was watched when he went to Germany and one day caught just as he was posting a letter in a code that was eventually deciphered. He was tried, convicted and shot. It was bad enough to lose a useful and disinterested agent, but it entailed besides the changing of a safe and simple code. R. was not pleased. But R. was not the man to let any desire for revenge stand in the way of his main object and it occurred to him that if Caypor was merely betraying his country for money it might be possible to get him to take more money to betray his employers. The fact that he had succeeded in delivering into their hands an agent of the Allies must seem to them an earnest of his good faith. He might be very useful. But R. had no notion what kind of man Caypor was: he had lived his shabby, furtive life obscurely, and the only photograph that existed of him was one taken for a passport. Ashenden's instructions were to get acquainted with Caypor and see whether there was any chance that he would work honestly for the British: if he thought there was, he was entitled to sound him out and if his suggestions were met with favor to make certain propositions. It was a task that needed tact and a knowledge of men. If on the other hand Ashenden came to the conclusion that Caypor could not be bought he was to watch and report his movements. The information he had obtained from Gustav was vague, but important; there was only one point in it that was interesting, and this was that the head of the German Intelligence Department in Berne was growing restive at Caypor's lack of activity. Caypor was asking for a higher salary and Major von P. had told him that he must earn it. It might be that he was urging him to go to

England. If he could be induced to cross the frontier Ashenden's work was done.

"How the devil do you expect *me* to persuade him to put his head in a noose?" asked Ashenden.

"It won't be a noose, it'll be a firing squad," said R.

"Caypor's clever."

"Well, be cleverer, then."

Ashenden made up his mind that he would take no steps to make Caypor's acquaintance, but allow the first advances to be made by him. If he was being pressed for results it must surely occur to him that it would be worth while to get into conversation with an Englishman who was employed in the Censorship Department. Ashenden was prepared with a supply of information that it could not in the least benefit the Central Powers to possess. With a false name and a false passport he had little fear that Caypor would guess that he was a British agent.

Ashenden did not have to wait long. Next day he was sitting in the doorway of the hotel, drinking a cup of coffee and already half asleep after a substantial *mittagessen*, when the Caypors came out of the dining room. Mrs. Caypor went upstairs and Caypor released his dog. The dog bounded along and in a friendly fashion leaped up against Ashenden.

"Come here, Fritzi," cried Caypor, and then to Ashenden: "I'm so sorry. But he's quite gentle."

"Oh, that's all right. He won't hurt me."

Caypor stopped at the doorway.

"He's a bull terrier. You don't often see them on the Continent." He seemed while he spoke to be taking Ashenden's measure; he called to the maid, "A coffee, please, *fräulein*. You've just arrived, haven't you?"

"Yes, I came yesterday."

"Really? I didn't see you in the dining room last night. Are you making a stay?"

"I don't know. I've been ill and I've come here to recuperate."

The maid came with the coffee and seeing Caypor talking to Ashenden put the tray on the table at which he was sitting. Caypor gave a laugh of faint embarrassment.

"I don't want to force myself upon you. I don't know why the maid put my coffee on your table."

"Please sit down," said Ashenden.

"It's very good of you. I've lived so long on the Continent that I'm always forgetting that my countrymen are apt to look upon it as confounded cheek if you talk to them. Are you English, by the way, or American?"

"English," said Ashenden.

Ashenden was by nature a very shy person, and he had in vain tried to cure himself of a failing that at his age was unseemly, but on occasion he knew how to make effective use of it. He explained now in a hesitating and awkward manner the facts that he had the day before told the landlady and that he was convinced she had already passed on to Caypor.

"You couldn't have come to a better place than Lucerne. It's an oasis of peace in this war-weary world. When you're here you might almost forget that there is such a thing as a war going on. That is why I've come here. I'm a journalist by profession."

"I couldn't help wondering if you wrote," said Ashenden, with an eager, timid smile.

It was clear that he had not learnt that "oasis of peace in a war-weary world" at the shipping office.

"You see, I married a German lady," said Caypor gravely.

"Oh, really?"

"I don't think anyone could be more patriotic than I am, I'm English through and through and I don't mind telling you that in my opinion the British Empire is the greatest instrument for good that the world has ever seen, but having a German wife I naturally see a good deal of the reverse of the medal. You don't have to tell me that the Germans have faults, but frankly I'm not prepared to admit that they're devils incarnate. At the beginning of the war my poor wife had a very rough time in England and I for one couldn't have blamed her if she'd felt rather bitter about it. Everyone thought she was a spy. It'll make you laugh when you know her. She's the typical German *hausfrau* who cares for nothing but her house and her husband and our only child Fritzi." Caypor fondled his dog and gave a little laugh. "Yes, Fritzi, you are our child, aren't you? Naturally it made my position very awkward. I was connected with some very important papers, and my editors weren't quite comfortable about it.

Well, to cut a long story short I thought the most dignified course was to resign and come to a neutral country till the storm blew over. My wife and I never discuss the war, though I'm bound to tell you that it's more on my account than hers; she's much more tolerant than I am and she's more willing to look upon this terrible business from my point of view than I am from hers."

"That is strange," said Ashenden. "As a rule women are so much more rabid than men."

"My wife is a very remarkable person. I should like to introduce you to her. By the way, I don't know if you know my name. Grantley Caypor."

"My name is Somerville," said Ashenden.

He told him then of the work he had been doing in the Censorship Department, and he fancied that into Caypor's eyes came a certain intentness. Presently he told him that he was looking for someone to give him conversation lessons in German so that he might rub up his rusty knowledge of the language; and as he spoke a notion flashed across his mind: he gave Caypor a look and saw that the same notion had come to him. It had occurred to them at the same instant that it would be a very good plan for Ashenden's teacher to be Mrs. Caypor.

"I asked our landlady if she could find me someone and she said she thought she could. I must ask her again. It ought not to be very hard to find a man who is prepared to come and talk German to me for an hour a day."

"I wouldn't take anyone on the landlady's recommendation," said Caypor. "After all, you want someone with a good north German accent and she only talks Swiss. I'll ask my wife if she knows anyone. My wife's a very highly educated woman and you could trust her recommendation."

"That's very kind of you."

Ashenden observed Grantley Caypor at his ease. He noticed how the small, gray-green eyes, which last night he had not been able to see, contradicted the red good-humored frankness of the face. They were quick and shifty, but when the mind behind them was seized by an unexpected notion they were suddenly still. It gave one a peculiar feeling of the working of the brain. They were not eyes that inspired confidence; Caypor did that with his jolly good-natured smile, the openness of his broad, weather-beaten face, his comfortable obesity and the cheeriness of his loud, deep voice. He was doing his best now to be agreeable. While Ashenden talked to him, a little shyly still but gaining confidence from that breezy, cordial manner capable of putting anyone at his ease, it intrigued him to remember that the man was a common spy. It gave a tang to his conversation to reflect that he had been ready to sell his country for no more than forty pounds a month. Ashenden had known Gomez, the young Spaniard whom Caypor had betrayed. He was a high-spirited youth, with a love of adventure, and he had undertaken his dangerous mission not for the money he earned by it, but from a passion for romance. It amused him to outwit the clumsy German and it appealed to his sense of the absurd to play a part in a shilling shocker. It was not very nice to think of him now six feet underground in a prison yard. He was young and he had a certain grace of gesture. Ashenden wondered whether Caypor had felt a qualm when he delivered him up to destruction.

"I suppose you know a little German?" asked Caypor, interested in the stranger.

"Oh, yes, I was a student in Germany, and I used to talk it fluently, but that is long ago and I have forgotten. I can still read it very comfortably."

"Oh, yes, I noticed you were reading a German book last night."

Fool! It was only a little while since he had told Ashenden that he had not seen him at dinner. He wondered whether Caypor had observed the slip. How difficult it was never to make one! Ashenden must be on his guard; the thing that made him most nervous was the thought that he might not answer readily enough to his assumed name of Somerville. Of course there was always the chance that Caypor had made the slip on purpose to see by Ashenden's face whether he noticed anything. Caypor got up.

"There is my wife. We go for a walk up one of the mountains every afternoon. I can tell you some charming walks. The flowers even now are lovely."

"I'm afraid I must wait till I'm a bit stronger," said Ashenden, with a little sigh.

He had naturally a pale face and never looked as robust as he was. Mrs. Caypor came downstairs and her husband joined her. They walked down the road, Fritzi bounding around them, and

Ashenden saw that Caypor immediately began to
speak with volubility. He was evidently telling his
wife the results of his interview with Ashenden.
Ashenden looked at the sun shining so gaily on
the lake; the shadow of a breeze fluttered the
green leaves of the trees; everything invited to a
stroll: he got up, went to his room and throwing
himself on his bed had a very pleasant sleep.

He went in to dinner that evening as the
Caypors were finishing, and on their way out of
the dining room Caypor stopped and asked him if
he would drink coffee with them. When Ashenden
joined them in the hall Caypor got up and intro-
duced him to his wife. She bowed stiffly and no
answering smile came to her face to respond to
Ashenden's civil greeting. It was not hard to see
that her attitude was definitely hostile. It put
Ashenden at his ease. She was a plainish woman,
nearing forty, with a muddy skin and vague features; her drab hair was arranged in a plait around
her head like that of Napoleon's Queen of Prussia;
and she was squarely built, plump rather than fat,
and solid. But she did not look stupid; she looked
on the contrary a woman of character and
Ashenden, who had lived enough in Germany to
recognize the type, was ready to believe that
though capable of doing the housework, cooking
the dinner and climbing a mountain, she might be
also prodigiously well-informed. She wore a white
blouse that showed a sunburned neck, a black
skirt and heavy walking boots. Caypor, addressing
her in English, told her in his jovial way, as though
she did not know it already, what Ashenden had

told him about himself. She listened grimly.

"I think you told me you understood German," said Caypor, his big red face wreathed in polite smiles but his little eyes darting about restlessly.

"Yes, I was for some time a student in Heidelberg."

"Really?" said Mrs. Caypor in English, an expression of faint interest for a moment chasing away the sullenness from her face. "I know Heidelberg very well. I was at school there for one year."

Her English was correct, but throaty, and the mouthing emphasis she gave her words was disagreeable. Ashenden was diffuse in praise of the old university town and the beauty of the neighborhood. She heard him, from the standpoint of her Teutonic superiority, with toleration rather than with enthusiasm.

"It is well known that the valley of the Neckar is one of the beauty places of the whole world," she said.

"I have not told you, my dear," said Caypor then, "that Mr. Somerville is looking for someone to give him conversation lessons while he is here. I told him that perhaps you could suggest a teacher."

"No, I know no one whom I could conscientiously recommend," she answered. "The Swiss accent is hateful beyond words. It could do Mr. Somerville only harm to converse with a Swiss."

"If I were in your place, Mr. Somerville, I would try and persuade my wife to give you lessons. She is, if I may say so, a very cultivated and highly educated woman."

"*Ach*, Grantley, I have not the time. I have my own work to do."

Ashenden saw that he was being given his opportunity. The trap was prepared and all he had to do was fall in. He turned to Mrs. Caypor with a manner that he tried to make shy, deprecating and modest.

"Of course it would be too wonderful if you would give me lessons. I should look upon it as a real privilege. Naturally I wouldn't want to interfere with your work. I am just here to get well, with nothing in the world to do, and I would suit my time entirely to your convenience."

He felt a flash of satisfaction pass from one to the other and in Mrs. Caypor's blue eyes he fancied that he saw a dark glow.

"Of course it would be a purely business arrangement," said Caypor. "There's no reason that my good wife shouldn't earn a little pin-money. Would you think ten francs an hour too much?"

"No," said Ashenden, "I should think myself lucky to get a first-rate teacher for that."

"What do you say, my dear? Surely you can spare an hour, and you would be doing this gentleman a kindness. He would learn that all Germans are not the devilish fiends that they think them in England."

On Mrs. Caypor's brow was an uneasy frown and Ashenden could not but think with apprehension of that hour's conversation a day that he was

going to exchange with her. Heaven only knew
how he would have to rack his brain for subjects of
discourse with that heavy and morose woman.
Now she made a visible effort.

"I shall be very pleased to give Mr. Somerville
conversation lessons."

"I congratulate you, Mr. Somerville," said
Caypor noisily. "You're in for a treat. When will
you start? Tomorrow at eleven?"

"That would suit me very well if it suits Mrs.
Caypor."

"Yes, that is as good an hour as another," she
answered.

Ashenden left them to discuss the happy out-
come of their diplomacy. But when, punctually at
eleven next morning, he heard a knock at his door
(for it had been arranged that Mrs. Caypor should
give him his lesson in his room) it was not
without trepidation that he opened it. It behooved
him to be frank, a trifle indiscreet, but obviously
wary of a German woman, sufficiently intelligent,
and impulsive. Mrs. Caypor's face was dark and
sulky. She plainly hated having anything to do
with him. But they sat down and she began,
somewhat peremptorily, to ask him questions
about his knowledge of German literature. She
corrected his mistakes with exactness and when
he put before her some difficulty in German
construction explained it with clearness and precision. It was obvious that though she hated
giving him a lesson she meant to give it conscientiously. She seemed to have not only an aptitude
for teaching, but a love of it, and as the hour went

on she began to speak with greater earnestness. It was already only by an effort that she remembered that he was a brutal Englishman. Ashenden, noticing the unconscious struggle within her, found himself not a little entertained; and it was with truth that, when later in the day Caypor asked him how the lesson had gone, he answered that it was highly satisfactory; Mrs. Caypor was an excellent teacher and a most interesting person.

"I told you so. She's the most remarkable woman I know."

And Ashenden had a feeling that when in his hearty, laughing way Caypor said this he was for the first time entirely sincere.

In a day or two Ashenden guessed that Mrs. Caypor was giving him lessons only in order to enable Caypor to arrive at a closer intimacy with him, for she confined herself strictly to matters of literature, music and painting; and when Ashenden, by way of experiment, brought the conversation around to the war, she cut him short.

"I think that is a topic that we had better avoid, Herr Somerville," she said.

She continued to give her lessons with the greatest thoroughness, and he had his money's worth, but every day she came with the same sullen face and it was only in the interest of teaching that she lost for a moment her instinctive dislike of him. Ashenden exercised in turn, but in vain, all his wiles. He was ingratiating, ingenuous, humble, grateful, flattering, simple and timid. She remained coldly hostile. She was a fanatic. Her patriotism was aggressive, but disinterested, and, obsessed with the notion of the superiority of all things German, she loathed England with a virulent hatred because in that country she saw the chief obstacle to their diffusion. Her ideal was a German world in which the rest of the nations under a hegemony greater than that of Rome should enjoy the benefits of German science and German art and German culture. There was in the conception a magnificent impudence that appealed to Ashenden's sense of humor. She was no fool. She had read much, in several languages, and she could talk of the books she had read with good sense. She had a knowledge of modern painting and modern music that not a little impressed Ashenden. It was amusing once to hear her before luncheon play one of those silvery little pieces of Debussy: she played it disdainfully because it was French and so light, but with an angry appreciation of its grace and gaiety. When Ashenden congratulated her she shrugged her shoulders.

"The decadent music of a decadent nation," she said. Then with powerful hands she struck the first resounding chords of a sonata by Beethoven; but she stopped. "I cannot play, I am out of practice, and you English, what do you know of music? You have not produced a composer since Purcell!"

"What do you think of that statement?" Ashenden, smiling, asked Caypor who was standing near.

"I confess its truth. The little I know of music my wife taught me. I wish you could hear her play when she is in practice." He put his fat hand, with its square, stumpy fingers, on her shoulder. "She can wring your heartstrings with pure beauty."

"*Dummer Kerl,*" she said, in a soft voice. "Stupid fellow," and Ashenden saw her mouth for a moment quiver, but she quickly recovered. "You English, you cannot paint, you cannot model, you cannot write music."

"Some of us can at times write pleasing verses," said Ashenden, with good humor, for it was not his business to be put out, and he did not know why, two lines occurring to him he said them:

> "*Whither, O splendid ship, thy white sails crowding,*
>   *Leaning across the bosom of the urgent West.*"

'Yes," said Mrs. Caypor, with a strange gesture, "you can write poetry. I wonder why."

And to Ashenden's surprise she went on, in her guttural English, to recite the next two lines of the poem he had quoted.

"Come, Grantley, *mittagessen* is ready, let us go into the dining room."

They left Ashenden reflective.

Ashenden admired goodness, but was not outraged by wickedness. People sometimes thought him heartless because he was more often interested in others than attached to them, and even in the few to whom he was attached his eyes saw with equal clearness the merits and the defects. When he liked people it was not because he was blind to their faults. He did not mind their faults but accepted them with a tolerant shrug of the shoulders, or because he ascribed to them excellencies that they did not possess; and since he judged his friends with candor they never disappointed him and so he seldom lost one. He asked from none more than he could give. He was able to pursue his study of the Caypors without prejudice and without passion.

Mrs. Caypor seemed to him more of a piece and therefore the easier of the two to understand. She obviously detested him; though it was so necessary for her to be civil to him, her antipathy was strong enough to wring from her now and then an expression of rudeness; and had she been safely able to do so she would have killed him without a qualm. But in the pressure of Caypor's chubby hand on his wife's shoulder and in the fugitive trembling of her lips Ashenden had divined that this unprepossessing woman and that mean fat man were joined together by a deep and sincere love. It was touching.

Ashenden assembled the observations that he had been making for the past few days and little things that he had noticed but to which he had attached no significance returned to him. It seemed to him that Mrs. Caypor loved her husband because she was of a stronger character than he and because she felt his dependence on her. She loved him for his admiration of her, and you might guess that till she met him this dumpy, plain woman with her dullness, good sense and want of humor could not have much enjoyed the admiration of men. She enjoyed his heartiness and his

noisy jokes, and his high spirits stirred her sluggish blood; he was a great big bouncing boy and he
would never be anything else and she felt like a
mother toward him. She had made him what he
was, and he was her man and she was his woman,
and she loved him, notwithstanding his weakness
(for with her clear head she must always have
been conscious of that), she loved him, *ach, was,*
as Isolde loved Tristan. But then there was the
espionage. Even Ashenden with all his tolerance
for human frailty could not but feel that to betray
your country for money is not a very pretty
proceeding. Of course she knew of it; indeed it
was probably through her that Caypor had first
been approached; he would never have undertak-
en such work if she had not urged him to it. She
loved him and she was an honest and an upright
woman. By what devious means had she persuad-
ed herself to force her husband to adopt so base
and dishonorable a calling? Ashenden lost himself
in a labyrinth of conjecture as he tried to piece
together the actions of her mind.

Grantley Caypor was another story. There was
little to admire in him, but at that moment
Ashenden was not looking for an object of admiration; but there was much that was singular and
much that was unexpected in that gross and
vulgar fellow. Ashenden watched with entertainment the suave manner in which the spy tried to
inveigle him in his toils. It was a couple of days
after his first lesson that Caypor after dinner, his
wife having gone upstairs, threw himself heavily
into a chair by Ashenden's side. His faithful Fritzi

came up to him and put his long muzzle with its black nose on his knee.

"He has no brain," said Caypor, "but a heart of gold. Look at those little pink eyes. Did you ever see anything so stupid? And what an ugly face, but what incredible charm!"

"Have you had him long?" asked Ashenden.

"I got him in 1914 just before the outbreak of war. By the way, what do you think of the news today? Of course my wife and I never discuss the war. You can't think what a relief to me it is to find a fellow-countryman to whom I can open my heart."

He handed Ashenden a cheap Swiss cigar and Ashenden, making a rueful sacrifice to duty, accepted it.

"Of course they haven't got a chance, the Germans," said Caypor, "not a dog's chance. I knew they were beaten the moment we came in."

His manner was earnest, sincere and confidential. Ashenden made a commonplace rejoinder.

"It's the greatest grief of my life that owing to my wife's nationality I was unable to do any war work. I tried to enlist the day war broke out, but they wouldn't have me on account of my age. But I don't mind telling you, if the war goes on much longer, wife or no wife, I'm going to do something. With my knowledge of languages I ought to be of some service in the Censorship Department. That's where you were, wasn't it?"

That was the mark at which he had been aiming and in answer now to his well-directed questions Ashenden gave him the information that he had already prepared. Caypor drew his chair a little nearer and dropped his voice.

"I'm sure you wouldn't tell me anything that anyone shouldn't know, but after all, these Swiss are absolutely pro-German and we don't want to give anyone the chance of overhearing."

Then he went on another tack. He told Ashenden a number of things that were of a certain secrecy.

"I wouldn't tell this to anybody else, you know, but I have one or two friends who are in pretty influential positions, and they know they can trust me."

Thus encouraged, Ashenden was a little more deliberately indiscreet and when they parted both had reason to be satisfied. Ashenden guessed that Caypor's typewriter would be kept busy next morning and that the extremely energetic major in Berne would shortly receive a most interesting report.

One evening, going upstairs after dinner, Ashenden passed an open bathroom. He caught sight of the Caypors.

"Come in," cried Caypor in his cordial way. "We're washing our Fritzi."

The bull terrier was constantly getting himself very dirty, and it was Caypor's pride to see him clean and white. Ashenden went in. Mrs. Caypor with her sleeves turned up and a large white apron was standing at one end of the bath, while Caypor, in a pair of trousers and a singlet, his fat, freckled arms bare, was soaping the wretched hound.

"We have to do it at night," he said, "because

the Fitzgeralds use this bath and they'd have a fit if they knew we washed the dog in it. We wait till they go to bed. Come along, Fritzi, show the gentleman how beautiful you behave when you have your face scrubbed."

The poor brute, woebegone but faintly wagging his tail to show that however foul was this operation performed on him he bore no malice to the god who did it, was standing in the middle of the bath in six inches of water. He was soaped all over and Caypor, talking the while, shampooed him with his great fat hands.

"Oh, what a beautiful dog he's going to be when he's as white as the driven snow. His master will be as proud as Punch to walk out with him and all the little lady dogs will say: good gracious, who's that beautiful aristocratic-looking bull terrier walking as though he owned the whole of Switzerland? Now stand still while you have your ears washed. You couldn't bear to go out into the street with dirty ears, could you? Like a nasty little Swiss schoolboy. *Noblesse oblige.* Now the black nose. Oh, and all the soap is going into his little pink eyes and they'll smart."

Mrs. Caypor listened to this nonsense with a good-humored sluggish smile on her broad, plain face, and presently gravely took a towel.

"Now he's going to have a ducking. Upsie-daisy."

Caypor seized the dog by the forelegs and ducked him once and ducked him twice. There was a struggle, a flurry and a splashing. Caypor lifted him out of the bath.

"Now go to mother and she'll dry you."

Mrs. Caypor sat down and, taking the dog between her strong legs, rubbed him till the sweat poured off her forehead. And Fritzi, a little shaken and breathless, but happy it was all over, stood white and shining.

"Blood will tell," cried Caypor exultantly. "He knows the names of no less than sixty-four of his ancestors, and they were all nobly born."

Ashenden was faintly troubled. He shivered a little as he walked upstairs.

Then, one Sunday, Caypor told him that he and his wife were going on an excursion and would eat their luncheon at some little mountain restaurant; and he suggested that Ashenden, each paying his share, should come with them. After three weeks at Lucerne Ashenden thought that his strength would permit him to venture the exertion. They started early, Mrs. Caypor businesslike in her walking boots and Tyrolese hat and alpenstock, and Caypor in stockings and plus-fours looking very British. The situation amused Ashenden and he was prepared to enjoy his day; but he meant to keep his eyes open. It was not inconceivable that the Caypors had discovered what he was and it would not do to go too near a precipice: Mrs. Caypor would not hesitate to give him a push and Caypor for all his jolliness was an ugly customer. But on the face of it there was nothing to mar Ashenden's pleasure in the golden morning. The air was fragrant. Caypor was full of conversation. He told funny stories. He was gay and jovial. The sweat rolled off his great red face and he laughed at himself because he was so fat. To Ashenden's astonishment he showed a peculiar knowledge of the mountain flowers. Once he went out of the way to pick one he saw a little distance from the path and brought it back to his wife. He looked at it tenderly.

"Isn't it lovely?" he cried, and his shifty gray-green eyes for a moment were as candid as a child's. "It's like a poem by Walter Savage Landor."

"Botany is my husband's favorite science," said Mrs. Caypor. "I laugh at him sometimes. He is devoted to flowers. Often when we have hardly had enough money to pay the butcher he has spent everything in his pocket to bring me a bunch of roses."

"*Qui fleurit sa maison fleurit son cœur*," said Grantley Caypor.

Ashenden had once or twice seen Caypor, coming in from a walk, offer Mrs. Fitzgerald a nosegay of mountain flowers with an elephantine courtesy that was not entirely displeasing; and what he had just learned added a certain significance to the pretty little action. His passion for flowers was genuine and when he gave them to the old Irish lady he gave her something he valued. It showed a real kindness of heart. Ashenden had always thought botany a tedious science, but Caypor, talking exuberantly as they walked along, was able to impart to it life and interest. He must have given it a good deal of study.

"I've never written a book," he said. "There are too many books already and any desire to write I

have is satisfied by the more immediately profit-
able and quite ephemeral composition of an article for a daily paper. But if I stay here much longer
I have half a mind to write a book about the wild
flowers of Switzerland. Oh, I wish you'd been here
a little earlier. They were marvelous. But one
wants to be a poet for that, and I'm only a poor
newspaper man."

It was curious to observe how he was able to
combine real emotion with false fact.

When they reached the inn, with its view of the
mountains and the lake, it was good to see the
sensual pleasure with which he poured down his
throat a bottle of ice-cold beer. You could not but
feel sympathy for a man who took so much delight
in simple things. They lunched deliciously off
scrambled eggs and mountain trout. Even Mrs.
Caypor was moved to an unwonted gentleness by
her surroundings; the inn was in an agreeably
rural spot, it looked like a picture of a Swiss châlet
in a book of early nineteenth century travels; and
she treated Ashenden with something less than
her usual hostility. When they arrived she had
burst into loud German exclamations on the beauty of the scene, and now, softened perhaps too by
food and drink, her eyes, dwelling on the grandeur
before her, filled with tears. She stretched out her
hand.

"It is dreadful and I am ashamed, notwithstanding this horrible and unjust war I can feel in my
heart at the moment nothing but happiness and
gratitude."

Caypor took her hand and pressed it and, an

unusual thing with him, addressing her in German, called her little pet names. It was absurd, but touching. Ashenden, leaving them to their emotions, strolled through the garden and sat down on a bench that had been prepared for the comfort of the tourist. The view was of course spectacular, but it captured you; it was like a piece of music that was obvious and meretricious, but for the moment shattered your self-control.

And as Ashenden lingered idly in that spot he pondered over the mystery of Grantley Caypor's treachery. If he liked strange people, he had found in him one who was strange beyond belief. It would be foolish to deny that he had amiable traits. His joviality was not assumed, he was without pretense a hearty fellow and he had real good nature. He was always ready to do a kindness. Ashenden had often watched him with the old Irish colonel and his wife who were the only other residents of the hotel; he would listen good-humoredly to the old man's tedious stories of the Egyptian war, and he was charming with her. Now that Ashenden had arrived at terms of some familiarity with Caypor he found that he regarded him less with repulsion than with curiosity. He did not think that he had become a spy merely for the money; he was a man of modest tastes and what he had earned in a shipping office must have sufficed to so good a manager as Mrs. Caypor; and after war was declared there was no lack of remunerative work for men over the military age. It might be that he was one of those men who prefer devious ways to straight for some intricate pleasure they get in fooling their fellows; and that he had turned spy, not from hatred of the country that had imprisoned him, not even from love of his wife, but from a desire to score off the big-wigs who never even knew of his existence. It might be that it was vanity that impelled him, a feeling that his talents had not received the recognition they merited, or just a puckish, impish desire to do mischief. He was a crook. It is true that only two cases of dishonesty had been brought home to him, but if he had been caught twice it might be surmised that he had often been dishonest without being caught. What did Mrs. Caypor think of this? They were so united that she must be aware of it. Did it make her ashamed, for her own uprightness surely none could doubt, or did she accept it as an inevitable kink in the man she loved? Did she do all she could to prevent it or did she close her eyes to something she could not help?

How much easier life would be if people were all black or all white and how much simpler it would be to act in regard to them! Was Caypor a good man who loved evil or a bad man who loved good? And how could such unreconcilable elements exist side by side and in harmony within the same heart? For one thing was clear, Caypor was disturbed by no gnawing of conscience; he did his mean and despicable work with gusto. He was a traitor who enjoyed his treachery. Though Ashenden had been studying human nature more or less consciously all his life, it seemed to him that he knew as little about it now in middle age as he had done when he was a child. Of course R. would have said to him: why the devil do you waste your time with such nonsense? The man's a dangerous spy and your business is to lay him by the heels.

That was true enough. Ashenden had decided that it would be useless to attempt to make any arrangement with Caypor. Though doubtless he would have no feeling about betraying his employers, he could certainly not be trusted. His wife's influence was too strong. Besides, notwithstanding what he had from time to time told Ashenden, he was in his heart convinced that the Central Powers must win the war, and he meant to be on the winning side. Well, then, Caypor must be laid by the heels, but how he was to effect that Ashenden had no notion. Suddenly he heard a voice.

"There you are. We've been wondering where you had hidden yourself."

He looked around and saw the Caypors strolling toward him. They were walking hand in hand.

"So this is what has kept you so quiet," said Caypor as his eyes fell on the view. "What a spot!"

Mrs. Caypor clasped her hands.

"*Ach Gott, wie schön!*" she cried. "*Wie schön.* When I look at that blue lake and those snowy mountains I feel inclined, like Goëthe's Faust, to cry to the passing moment: tarry."

"This is better than being in England with the excursions and alarums of war, isn't it?" said Caypor.

"Much," said Ashenden.

"By the way, did you have any difficulty in getting out?"

"No, not the smallest."

"I'm told they make rather a nuisance of themselves at the frontier nowadays."

"I came through without the smallest difficulty. I don't fancy they bother much about the English. I thought the examination of passports was quite perfunctory."

A fleeting glance passed between Caypor and his wife. Ashenden wondered what it meant. It would be strange if Caypor's thoughts were occupied with the chances of a journey to England at the very moment when he was himself reflecting on its possibility. In a little while Mrs. Caypor suggested that they had better be starting back and they wandered together in the shade of trees down the mountain paths.

Ashenden was watchful. He could do nothing (and his inactivity irked him) but wait with his eyes open to seize the opportunity that might present itself. A couple of days later an incident occurred that made him certain something was in the wind. In the course of his morning lesson Mrs. Caypor remarked:

"My husband has gone to Geneva today. He had some business to do there."

"Oh," said Ashenden, "will he be long?"

"No, only two days."

It is not everyone who can tell a lie and Ashenden had the feeling, he hardly knew why, that Mrs. Caypor was telling one then. Her manner perhaps was not quite as indifferent as you would have expected when she was mentioning a fact that could be of no interest to Ashenden. It flashed across his mind that Caypor had been summoned to Berne to see the redoubtable head of the German secret service. When he had the chance he said casually to the waitress:

"A little less work for you to do, *fräulein*. I hear that Herr Caypor has gone to Berne."

"Yes. But he'll be back tomorrow."

That proved nothing, but it was something to go upon. Ashenden knew in Lucerne a Swiss who was willing on emergency to do odd jobs and, looking him up, asked him to take a letter to Berne. It might be possible to pick up Caypor and trace his movements. Next day Caypor appeared once more with his wife at the dinner table, but merely nodded to Ashenden and afterwards both went straight upstairs. They looked troubled. Caypor, as a rule so animated, walked with bowed shoulders and looked neither to the right nor to the left. Next morning Ashenden received a reply to his letter: Caypor had seen Major von P. It was possible to guess what the major had said to him. Ashenden well knew how rough he could be: he was a hard man and brutal, clever and unscrupulous, and he was not accustomed to mince his words. They were tired of paying Caypor a salary to sit still in Lucerne and do nothing; the time was come for him to go to England. Guesswork? Of course it was guesswork, but in that trade it mostly was: you had to deduce the animal from its jawbone. Ashenden knew from Gustav that the Germans wanted to send someone to England. He drew a long breath; if Caypor went he would have to get busy.

When Mrs. Caypor came in to give him his lesson she was dull and listless. She looked tired and her mouth was set obstinately. It occurred to Ashenden that the Caypors had spent most of the night talking. He wished he knew what they had said. Did she urge him to go or did she try to dissuade him? Ashenden watched them again at luncheon. Something was the matter, for they hardly spoke to one another and as a rule they found plenty to talk about. They left the room early, but when Ashenden went out he saw Caypor sitting in the hall by himself.

"Hulloa," he cried jovially, but surely the effort was patent, "how are you getting on? I've been to Geneva."

"So I heard," said Ashenden.

"Come and have your coffee with me. My poor wife's got a headache. I told her she'd better go and lie down." In his shifty green eyes was an expression that Ashenden could not read. "The fact is, she's rather worried, poor dear; I'm thinking of going to England."

Ashenden's heart gave a sudden leap against his ribs, but his face remained impassive.

"Oh, are you going for long? We shall miss you."

"To tell you the truth, I'm fed up with doing nothing. The war looks as though it were going on for years and I can't sit here indefinitely. Besides, I can't afford it, I've got to earn my living. I may have a German wife, but I am an Englishman, hang it all, and I want to do my bit. I could never face my friends again if I just stayed here in ease and comfort till the end of the war and never attempted to do a thing to help the country. My wife takes her German point of view and I don't mind telling you she's a bit upset. You know what women are."

Now Ashenden knew what it was that he saw in Caypor's eyes. Fear. It gave him a nasty turn. Caypor didn't want to go to England, he wanted to stay safely in Switzerland; Ashenden knew now what the major had said to him when he went to see him in Berne. He had got to go or lose his salary. What was it that his wife had said when he told her what had happened? He had wanted her to press him to stay, but it was plain she hadn't done that; perhaps he had not dared tell her how frightened he was. To her he had always been gay, bold, adventurous and devil-may-care; and now, the prisoner of his own lies, he had not found it in him to confess himself the mean and sneaking coward he was.

"Are you going to take your wife with you?" asked Ashenden.

"No, she'll stay here."

It had been arranged very neatly. Mrs. Caypor would receive his letters and forward the information they contained to Berne.

"I've been out of England so long that I don't quite know how to set about getting war work. What would you do in my place?"

"I don't know; what sort of work are you thinking of?"

"Well, you know, I imagine I could do the same thing as you did. I wonder if there's anyone in the

Censorship Department that you could give me a letter of introduction to."

It was only by a miracle that Ashenden saved himself from showing by a smothered cry or by a broken gesture how startled he was; but not by Caypor's request, but what had just dawned upon him. What an idiot he had been! He had been disturbed by the thought that he was wasting his time at Lucerne, he was doing nothing, and though in fact, as it turned out, Caypor was going to England, it was due to no cleverness of his. He could take to himself no credit for the result. And now he saw that he had been put in Lucerne, told how to describe himself and given the proper information, so that what actually had occurred should occur. It would be a wonderful thing for the German secret service to get an agent into the Censorship Department; and by a happy accident there was Grantley Caypor, the very man for the job, on friendly terms with someone who worked there. What a bit of luck! It was a trap of that devilish R., and the grim major at Berne had fallen into it. Ashenden had done his work just by sitting still and doing nothing. He almost laughed as he thought what a fool R. had made of him.

"I was on very good terms with the chief of my department. I could give you a note to him if you liked."

"That would be just the thing."

"But of course I must give the facts. I must say I've met you here and only known you a fortnight."

"Of course. But you'll say what else you can for me, won't you?"

"Oh, certainly."

"I don't know yet if I can get a visa. I'm told they're rather fussy."

"I don't see why. I shall be very sick if they refuse me one when I want to go back."

"I'll go and see how my wife is getting on," said Caypor, suddenly getting up. "When will you let me have that letter?"

"Whenever you like. Are you going at once?"

"As soon as possible."

Caypor left him. Ashenden waited in the hall for a quarter of an hour so that there should appear in him no sign of hurry. Then he went upstairs and prepared various communications. In one he informed R. that Caypor was going to England; in another he made arrangements through Berne that wherever Caypor applied for a visa it should be granted to him without question; and these he dispatched forthwith. When he went down to dinner he handed Caypor a cordial letter of introduction.

Next day but one Caypor left Lucerne.

Ashenden waited. He continued to have his hour's lesson with Mrs. Caypor and under her conscientious tuition began now to speak German with ease. They talked of Goëthe and Winckelmann, of art and life and travel. Fritzi sat quietly by her chair.

"He misses his master," she said, pulling his ears. "He only really cares for him. He suffers me only as belonging to him."

After his lesson Ashenden went every morning to Cook's to ask for his letters. It was here that all communications were addressed to him. He could not move till he received instructions, but R. could be trusted not to leave him idle long; and meanwhile there was nothing for him to do but have patience. Presently he received a letter from the consul in Geneva to say that Caypor had there applied for his visa and had set out for France. Having read this Ashenden went on for a little stroll by the lake and on his way back happened to see Mrs. Caypor coming out of Cook's office. He guessed that she was having her letters addressed there too. He went up to her.

"Have you had news of Herr Caypor?" he asked her.

"No," she said. "I suppose I could hardly expect to yet."

He walked along by her side. She was disappointed, but not yet anxious; she knew how irregular at that time was the post. But next day during his lesson he could not but see that she was impatient to have done with it. The post was delivered at noon and at five minutes to she looked at her watch and him. Though Ashenden knew very well that no letter would ever come for her he had not the heart to keep her on tenterhooks.

"Don't you think that's enough for the day? I'm sure you want to go down to Cook's," he said.

"Thank you. That is very amiable of you."

Later he went there himself and he found her standing in the middle of the office. Her face was distraught. She addressed him wildly.

"My husband promised to write from Paris. I am sure there is a letter for me, but these stupid people say there's nothing. They're so careless, it's a scandal."

Ashenden did not know what to say. While the clerk was looking through the bundle to see if there was anything for him she came up to the desk again.

"When does the next post come in from France?" she asked.

"Sometimes there are letters about five."

"I'll come then."

She turned and walked rapidly away. Fritzi followed her with his tail between his legs. There was no doubt of it, already the fear had seized her that something was wrong. Next morning she looked dreadful; she could not have closed her eyes all night; and in the middle of the lesson she started up from her chair.

"You must excuse me, Herr Somerville, I cannot give you a lesson today. I am not feeling well."

Before Ashenden could say anything she had flung nervously from the room, and in the evening he got a note from her to say that she regretted that she must discontinue giving him conversation lessons. She gave no reason. Then Ashenden saw no more of her; she ceased coming in to meals; except to go morning and afternoon to Cook's she spent apparently the whole day in her room. Ashenden thought of her sitting there hour after hour with that hideous fear gnawing at her heart. Who could help feeling sorry for her? The

time hung heavy on his hands too. He read a good
deal and wrote a little, he hired a canoe and went
for long leisurely paddles on the lake; and at last
one morning the clerk at Cook's handed him a
letter. It was from R. It had all the appearance of a
business communication, but between the lines
he read a good deal.

Dear Sir, it began, *The goods, with accompany-
ing letter, dispatched by you from Lucerne have
been duly delivered. We are obliged to you for
executing our instructions with such promptness.*

It went on in this strain. R. was exultant.
Ashenden guessed that Caypor had been arrested
and by now had paid the penalty of his crime. He
shuddered. He remembered a dreadful scene.
Dawn. A cold, gray dawn, with a drizzling rain
falling. A man, blindfolded, standing against a
wall, an officer very pale giving an order, a volley,
and then a young soldier, one of the firing party,
turning around and holding on to his gun for
support, vomiting. The officer turning paler still,
and he, Ashenden, feeling dreadfully faint. How
terrified Caypor must have been! It was awful
when the tears ran down their faces. Ashenden
shook himself. He went to the ticket office and
obedient to his orders bought himself a ticket for
Geneva.

As he was waiting for his change Mrs. Caypor
came in. He was shocked at the sight of her. She
was blowsy and disheveled and there were heavy
rings around her eyes. She was deathly pale. She
staggered up to the desk and asked for a letter. The
clerk shook his head.

"I'm sorry, madam, there's nothing yet."

"But look, look. Are you sure? Please look again."

The misery in her voice was heart-rending. The clerk with a shrug of the shoulders took out the letters from a pigeonhole and sorted them once more.

"No, there's nothing, madam."

She gave a hoarse cry of despair and her face was distorted with anguish.

"Oh, God, oh, God," she moaned.

She turned away, the tears streaming from her weary eyes, and for a moment she stood there like a blind man groping and not knowing which way to go. Then a fearful thing happened. Fritzi, the bull terrier, sat down on his haunches and threw back his head and gave a long, long melancholy howl. Mrs. Caypor looked at him with terror; her eyes seemed really to start from her head. The doubt, the gnawing doubt that had tortured her during those dreadful days of suspense, was a doubt no longer. She knew. She staggered blindly into the street.

Code No. 2

Edgar Wallace

The Secret Service never call themselves anything so melodramatic. If they speak at all, it is vaguely of "The Department"—not even "The Intelligence Department," you will note. It is a remarkable department, however, and not the least of the remarkable men who served—in a minor capacity, it is true—was Schiller.

He was an inventive young Swiss with a passion for foreign languages. He knew all the bad men in London—bad from the violently political standpoint—and was useful to the Chief Secretary (Intelligence), though Bland and the big men . . . well, they didn't dislike him, but they sort of . . . I don't know how to put it.

Watch a high-spirited horse pass a scrap of white paper on the road. He doesn't exactly shy, but he looks at the flapping thing very doubtfully.

Schiller was never in the Big Game, though he tried his best to get there. But the Big Game was played by men who "chew ciphers in the cradle," as Bland put it.

In some mysterious way Schiller got to know that Reggie Batten had been shot dead whilst extracting the mobilization orders of the 14th Bavarian Corps from a safe in Munich. This was in 1911, and the sad occurrence was described as an "aviation accident."

The Munich military authorities took Reggie's body up in an aeroplane and dropped it . . . and the Munich newspapers gave poor Reggie some beautiful notices, and said that the funeral would be at two o'clock, and they hoped that all his loving friends would gather round. Such of his unsuspecting acquaintances as did gather were arrested and searched, their lodgings and baggage ransacked, and they in due course were most incontinently sent across the frontier.

Bland, who was in Munich, did not attend the funeral; in fact, he left the beer city without lingering unnecessarily.

He was back in town only a day when Schiller asked for an interview.

Bland, square-chinned, clean-shaven, and wholly impassive, heard particulars of Schiller's application and laughed.

"You are altogether wrong in your view of Mr. Batten," he said. "He was unconnected with this department, and his death was due to a very deplorable accident. Therefore I cannot give you his job."

Schiller heard and bowed.

"I have been misinformed, sir," he said politely.

He went to work in another way and made a carefully planned attack upon the Chief Secretary,

who had reached that delicate stage of a man's
career which is represented by the interregnum
between the end of a period of usefulness and the
consciousness of the fact.

Sir John Grandor had been in his time the
greatest Intelligence man in Europe, but now—he
still talked of wireless telegraphy as "a wonderful
invention."

Yet Sir John was Chief, and a fairly shrewd
Chief. His seal of office was Code No. 2, which no
mortal eye had seen save his. It lay on the bottom
shelf of the safe between steel-bound covers, sheet
after sheet of close writing in his own neat hand.

No. 2 Code is a very secret one. It is the code
which the big agents employ. It is not printed, nor
are written copies circulated, but it is learned
under the tuition of the Chief himself. The men
who know Code No. 2 do not boast of their
knowledge, because their lives hang upon a thread
— even in peace time.

Schiller could never be a big agent. For one
thing, he was a naturalized foreign subject and the
big men are nationals, trained to the Game from
the day they enter the Office. They are educated
men, condemned for life to dissociate themselves
from the land of their birth; and who they are, or
where they live is known only to three men, two
of whom have no official existence.

Sir John liked Schiller and did many things for
him. He told him stories of his past adventures
and Schiller listened attentively. In the course of
one of these post-prandial discussions—he was a
most presentable young man, and Sir John fre-

quently took him home to dinner—Schiller casually mentioned Code No. 2. He spoke of it with
easy familiarity, and Sir John discussed the code in
general terms. He told his guest how it was kept in
the special safe, how it was made up on the
loose-leaf system, and how it was a nuisance
because it was always in disorder because he had
to consult it every day, and invariably replaced the
sheets he had been using on the top, irrespective
of their alphabetical right to that position.

The young man had innocently suggested that
he should come to Sir John's office every night and
sort the papers out, but the old man smiled
benevolently and had said he thought not.

Bland summoned Grigsby to his office one day,
and that florid young man came promptly.

"This fellow Schiller is bothering me," said
Bland in the low tones which are almost second
nature in the Service. "He's a smart fellow and
very useful, but I mistrust him."

"He has a blameless record," said the other,
staring out of the window, "and he knows little of
the bigger things. Sir John is a ditherer, but he's
close enough. What is worrying you now?"

Bland strode up and down the room.

"He's inventing a new wireless receiver," he
said, "and he's got the old man interested. He
works all day at it in his room, and at night he
carries it down to Sir John's office, where it is
most religiously locked in the safe.

"Of course, it is absurd to imagine that the
box—it is about the size of a biscuit tin—can
contain anything with human intelligence and get

out in an air-tight safe and walk around, or go squinting at the code but, somehow, I don't like it."

Grigsby chuckled.

"It's a new one on me," he confessed. "I'm not denying that Schiller isn't clever; he invented a draft excluder for my room which is a model of ingenuity, but I can hardly imagine a wireless receiver which reads and transmits a code from the interior of a steel safe."

But Bland was not convinced.

He sent for Mary Prince. She was on holiday in Devonshire, but came at once to town; a straight slip of a girl—she looked eighteen, though in truth she was ten years older—with the loveliest smile in the world, a pair of appraising gray eyes, and a mouth which, in repose, was a little inclined to droop.

"Sorry to disturb you on your holiday," said Bland, "but I want Schiller kept under observation. Next week you will be discharged from the Department for neglect of duty. You will retire with a grievance, and you will tell Schiller, whom you will continue to meet, that I am a beast and that I lose a great deal of money backing race horses. I will have a few bookmakers' accounts prepared for you, which you will show discreetly."

"Is he to blackmail you?" she asked.

Bland shook his head.

"If he is all I think he is, he will not. No, he might give you confidence for confidence. So long."

And Mary, with a nod, went out.

Schiller's invention took an unconscionable time to develop. Yet he was enthusiastic over its possibilities and inspired the Chief with some of his enthusiasm. He worked in his spare time at the machine, and regularly every evening at five minutes to six he would carry his heavy box to the Chief's office, solemnly deposit his burden on the iron grill which formed the one shelf of the safe, and watch the locking up with a jealous eye.

And Mary Prince had nothing to report. Three days before the fatal 1st of August which brought so much destruction and misery to Europe, Bland, who had been working day and night in the interest of his department, went up to Schiller's room to question him regarding the *bona fides* of a certain Antonio Malatesta, suspected of being an agent of the Central Powers. Bland very seldom visited the offices of his subordinates, but on this occasion his phone was out of order.

He found the door locked and knocked impatiently. Presently it was opened by the smiling Schiller. The table was covered with a litter of wire, electric batteries, tools, and screws; but of the great wireless receiver there was no sign.

"You are looking for my wonder-box, sir?" said Schiller. "She is in my safe. Soon I will give you the most remarkable demonstration! Even today I caught a signal from the Admiralty through a closed window."

But Bland was not listening.

He stood erect, his nose in the air, sniffing.

There was a faint, sweetish smell—a scent of

camphor and something else. Schiller watched him through narrowed eyes.

"H'm," said Bland and, turning on his heel, he left the room.

A telegram lay on the table. It had been delivered in his brief absence:

"Schiller is agent in Central European pay. He is head of cryptogram department. Have proof. MARY."

Bland pulled open the drawer of his desk, took out an automatic, raced through the door, and took the stairs two at a time.

Schiller's door was open, but he had gone.

He had not passed out through the lobby or the front entrance of the building, but a commissionaire on duty at the side door had seen him pass and had heard him hail a cab.

Bland went back to his office and put through a phone call to the police:

"Watch all railway stations and docks. Arrest and detain Augustus Schiller."

He described him briefly, but with a sure touch.

"It is very lamentable," said Sir John, really troubled, "but I can't think he has taken away anything of importance. Has he removed his invention?"

"I have that all right, Sir John," said Bland grimly, "and tonight with your permission I am going to see what happens."

"But surely you don't think—?"

Bland nodded. "I haven't monkeyed with it at all, but I've listened very carefully through a microphone and there is no doubt that it contains a clockwork mechanism. It is almost silent, but I have detected the sound. I suggest that we place the box where it is usually put, leave the safe door open, and watch."

Sir John frowned. All this seemed a reflection on his judgment and, as such, was to be resented. But he was too loyal a man in the Service to which he had given forty-five years of his life to allow his injured vanity to come before his public duty.

At six o'clock the box was placed in the safe.

"Is that where it was always put?" asked Bland.

"I generally—in fact invariably—put it on the iron grid."

"Just above Code 2, I see, sir."

The Chief Secretary frowned again, but this time in an effort of thought.

"That is true," he said slowly. "Once, I remember, when the box was placed a little to one side Schiller pushed it to the center, which I thought was a little impertinent of him."

The two men drew up a couple of armchairs and seated themselves before the safe.

Their vigil promised to be a long one.

Eight, nine, ten o'clock passed, and nothing happened.

"I think it's rather ridiculous, don't you?" asked Sir John testily, as the clock chimed quarter to eleven.

"It seems so," said Bland doggedly, "but I want to see—good God—look!"

Sir John gasped.

Immediately beneath the box was Code 2, enclosed in a leather binder, the edges of which were bound, for durability's sake, with a thin ribbon of steel.

Now, slowly the cover of the book was rising. It jerked up a little, then fell, leapt again and fell back, as though there were something inside which was struggling to get free. Then of a sudden the cover opened and remained stiffly erect, forming, with the contents, the letter L, the upright of which was the cover.

There was a "click," and the interior of the safe was illuminated with a soft greenish radiance. It threw a glow upon the top page of the code which lasted for nearly a minute. Then it died away and the cover of the book fell.

"Phew!" whistled Bland.

He lifted the black box carefully from the safe and carried it to Sir John's desk, examined the bottom of the box with a long and patient scrutiny, then set it down.

"Code No. 2 is in the hands of the enemy, sir," he said.

It was daylight when he finished his investigations. Half the box was taken up by accumulators. They supplied the current which, operating through a powerful magnet, lifted the cover of the code-book. They gave the light to the wonderful little mercurial-vapor lamps, which afforded the concealed camera just enough light to make an effective exposure.

"The little clockwork arrangement that sets the time for the machine to work and switches the current on and off is, of course, simple," said Bland. "It probably opens and closes the shutters which hide the lens and the lamp and the magnet. I suspected the camera when I smelled the film in his room."

Sir John, white and haggard, nodded.

"Get me out of this as well as you can, Bland," he said gruffly. "I'll retire at the end of the year. I'm an old man."

He walked to the door and pushed with his fingers on the handle.

"There are thirty men's lives in Schiller's keeping," he said. "Their names and addresses are in that book. I suppose he got through the book. I am so careless that I changed the order of the pages almost every day, and the devil has been at work for nine months. He ought to have worked through the book by now, for there was a different sheet on top every time."

"I'll do my best, sir," said Bland.

Schiller was away—and safely away—before war was declared. He was seen in Holland and was traced to Cologne. There was no possibility of changing the code, and messages were already coming through from agents.

Bland took a bold step. Through a man in Denmark he got into communication with Schiller and offered to make a deal. But Schiller was not selling. In the telegraphed words of the emissary whom Bland had sent:

"Schiller is receiving an enormous fee from enemy government for decoding wireless messages that your agents are sending. He alone knows the code."

Nothing daunted, Bland again got into communication with the traitor, offering him an enormous sum if he would consent to return to a neutral country and retain his secret.

"Meet me in Holland, and I will fix everything," his message ended. It elicited a reply which was characteristic of the ingenious master-spy:

"Come to Belgium and I will arrange."

A mad suggestion, for Belgium was now enemy ground, but Bland took his life in his hands, and a long glass dagger in his overnight bag, and left the same night for the Continent.

Bland went into Belgium by the back door and made a laborious way to Brussels. It would not be in the national interest to explain the means and methods he employed to make his entry into that carefully guarded land, but it is sufficient to say that he met Schiller, looking very prosperous, in the *estaminet* of the Gold Lion at Hazbruille, a small village on the Ghent-Lille Road.

"You are a very brave man, Mr. Bland," complimented Schiller, "and I wish I could oblige you in what you wish. Unfortunately, I cannot."

"Then why did you bring me here?" asked Bland.

The other looked at him curiously.

"I have a certain code," he said quietly. "I have it complete with certain exceptions: there are three pages missing. What do you want for them?"

Here was a staggerer for a smaller man than Bland.

"That is a fair question," he said, calmness itself, "but what is the particular code you are buying?"

"No. 2," said the other. "I thought . . ."

Bland interrupted him.

"No. 2 Code?" he said, sipping his bock (he was for the time being a Belgium peasant). "Of course, that's rubbish. Neither you nor I know No. 2 Code; the code you stole was No. 3."

Schiller smiled superiorly.

"When you get back to London," he said, "ask your Chief whether 'Agate' does not mean 'Transports loading at Borkum.' "

"You might have got hold of that particular word by accident," said Bland grudgingly.

"Ask him if 'Optique' does not mean 'Emperor has gone to Dresden,' " persisted the calm Schiller.

Bland looked around the room thoughtfully.

"You know a great deal, my friend," he said.

The woman who managed the *estaminet* came in a little later and found Bland puffing slowly at a rank cigar, his elbows on the table, a half-emptied bock before him.

The woman glanced at Schiller with a smile.

"He's tired," said Bland, emptying the bock. "Let him sleep on. And don't let the flies disturb him," he added humorously.

Schiller lay sideways on the bench at which Bland was sitting, his face to the wall, and over his head was a coarse blue handkerchief.

"He will not be disturbed," said Madame, and pocketed the five-sou tip that Bland gave her with a grateful smirk.

"When he wakes," said Bland at the door, "tell him I have gone on to Ghent."

Three hours later a German *landsturm* soldier,

who had come for his evening coffee, whisked away the handkerchief which covered the sleeper's face, and stammered:

"*Gott!*"

For Schiller was dead, and had been dead for three hours. It took even the doctor quite a long time to discover the blade of the glass dagger in his heart.

A week after this Bland was dressing for dinner in his West End flat, and had reached the patience stage of bow-tying, when his valet informed him that Grigsby had called.

"I told him you were dressing, sir," said Taylor, "but Mr. Grigsby is that full of his horse winning the Gatwick steeplechase that he won't take 'No' for an answer."

Taylor was a privileged person, and was permitted to be critical even of Bland's friends. Taylor was an ideal servant from his master's point of view, being simple and garrulous. To a man in Bland's profession garrulity in a servant was a virtue because it kept the employer always on his guard, never allowed him the delusion of safety or the luxury of indiscretion. Moreover, one knew what a garrulous servant was thinking and, through the medium of secret agents, what he was saying.

"Show him up here," said Bland after a while.

Mr. Grigsby came noisily into the dressing room, though his greeting of Bland was a little cold.

"I've a bone to pick with you," he said. "What the devil have you been saying to Lady Greenholm about me? You know my feeling about Alice—"

"Wait a moment, please," said Bland sharply, and turned to his servant. "Taylor, you can go to the General Post Office with the letter you will find on the hall stand."

Mr. Grigsby waited until he heard the door of the flat close, then walked into the passage and shot the bolt of the front door.

He came back to where Bland was standing with his back to the fire, his hands thrust into his trouser pockets.

"You're sure he had No. 2?" he asked.

Bland nodded.

Grigsby bit his lips thoughtfully.

"It isn't worth while worrying about how he got it—now," he said. "The question is, who will get it next?"

Bland opened a cigar case, bit off the end of a cigar, and lit up before he replied.

"What news have you at this end?" he asked. "I was across the border before they discovered his death; naturally, I've heard nothing except what our Amsterdam man told me."

"The code is in London," said Grigsby briefly. "As soon as he was dead a cablegram was sent to Valparaiso by the authorities in Brussels. It was addressed to a man named Von Hooch—probably a third party. Here it is—"

He took out a pocketbook and laid a slip of paper on the table. The message was short and was in Spanish:

SCHILLER'S LONDON LODGING.

"It's rather puzzling," said Bland. "Schiller wouldn't have written the code out—he was too clever for that. And yet he must have given the authorities a guarantee that the secret would not be lost with his death. It has probably been arranged that he should tell some person agreed upon—in this case a man in South America—in what manner the code was hidden. The exact locale he left until his death, probably sealed up amongst his private papers."

"That's a sound theory," said Grigsby. "He told you nothing more—"

Bland shook his head.

"I had to kill him, of course," he said with a note of regret. "It was pretty unpleasant, but the lives of thirty good men were in his holding. He probably knew where they were stationed."

"And the man who comes after will also know," said the other grimly. "We start tonight to make a very scientific search of his lodgings."

But the flat in Soho Square yielded no profit.

For the greater part of a fortnight three of the smartest Intelligence men—including Lecomte from the French department—probed and searched, slitting furniture, pulling up floors, and dismantling cupboards.

And the result was a negative one.

"I'll swear it is there," said Bland dejectedly. "We've overlooked something. Where is Mary Prince?"

"She's at the Chief Censor's. She has an office there," explained Grigsby.

"Ask her to come over."

Mary came in some triumph.

"I thought you'd send for me," she said. "I could have saved you such a lot of trouble!"

Bland was all apologies.

"I've neglected you terribly, Mary," he smiled. "Do you know, I haven't seen you since you sent me the wire about Schiller?"

She nodded.

"I know that. Schiller's dead, isn't he?"

"How did you know?"

She shrugged her shoulders.

"One reads things in the Censor's office—innocent letters from Holland, with messages written between the lines in formic acid and milk which becomes quite visible if you use the correct formulae. Mr. Schiller was a remarkable man; and his father was one of the greatest scholars Switzerland has produced, though he was blind. What do you want of me now?"

Bland explained briefly. The girl knew of Code No. 2 and the secrecy which surrounded it, and realized the urgency of the situation.

"By the way, how did you know he was an enemy agent?" he asked.

"I discovered *his* code," she replied cryptically.

Accompanied by the two men she went to the flat in Soho Square. The flooring had been replaced and the rooms were habitable again. Mary made a tour through the flat, then she returned to the big dining room.

"This is the room where the code is," she said decisively.

It was a cheerful apartment, papered in a rich

brown. A broad dado of a simple design belted the walls, and the wainscotting had been painted a chocolate color to harmonize with the paper. From the ceiling hung an electric light fitting, and Mary glanced at it.

"We've had that down," said Bland, "and the wainscot has been taken out, but we've found nothing."

"Will you leave me alone here for a few minutes?" asked the girl.

The two men withdrew, but they were hardly out of the room before she followed, her eyes blazing with the joy of discovery.

"Got it!" she laughed. "Oh, I knew—I knew!"

"Where is it?" demanded the astonished Bland.

"Wait," she said eagerly. "When do you expect your South American visitor?"

"Tomorrow. Of course, the room will be guarded and he will have no chance of searching."

Her eyes were still dancing when she nodded.

"We shall see—tomorrow. I fancy you will have a very frank visitor from Valparaiso, and when he comes I want you to send for me."

"What on earth—"

"Wait, wait, please! What will he say?" She closed her eyes and frowned. "I can tell you his name. It is Raymond Viztelli—"

"You knew this all along?" asked the astonished Grigsby, but she shook her head.

"I knew it when I went into the room," she said, "but now I am guessing. I think he will offer to help you discover the code, and he will tell you there is a secret panel in the wall, and that it will take days and days to make the discovery. And I think he will ask you to be present when he makes his search."

"He needn't ask that," said Bland unpleasantly. "I think you're very mysterious, Mary, but I've a kind of feeling that you're right."

She had a few questions to ask the janitor of the building before she left.

"Mr. Schiller did all his own decorations in the dining room, didn't he?"

"Yes, miss," said the man. "A regular feller he was for potterin' about with a pastepot or a paint-brush."

"And he has paid his rent in advance?"

"That's right, miss."

"And said that nothing was to be done to the flat till he came back?"

"His very words!" said the caretaker.

"I thought so," said Mary.

At ten o'clock next morning a card was brought to Bland. It was inscribed:

SENOR X. BERTRAMO DA SILVA

and written in a corner, "of Valparaiso."

Bland pressed a bell, and in a few minutes Grigsby and the girl came in.

"He's come," said Bland shortly, and handed her the card.

The visitor was shown in. He was a dapper little man with a pointed beard and he spoke excellent English. Moreover, after the preliminaries he plunged straight into the heart of his subject.

"I am going to be very frank with you, Mr. Bland," he began; and Bland, shooting a swift glance at the girl, saw the laughter in her eyes.

"I was for some time an agent of the Central Powers. I tell you this because I wish you to clearly understand my position," he went on. "Safe in South America, I thought no call would be made upon my services. A few weeks ago, however, I received a cablegram which was intercepted by the British authorities.

"I had known, of course, that in certain eventualities I might be asked to come to England to search for certain documents and that I should learn the place where they were hidden by telegram. That telegram came—I am here!"

He flung up his arms dramatically.

"I came straight to you on my arrival. I tell you frankly why I came, because I decided, the night before I reached Plymouth, that the game was not worth the candle. I will assist you as far as possible to discover the documents and then I will, if you will allow me, return to South America."

It was all very amazing to Bland. The man had said almost all that Mary had predicted he would say. He looked at the girl again, and she nodded.

"You understand that your search—" began Bland.

"Will be under the eyes of the police?" interrupted the man from Valparaiso. "I would prefer it."

"You would like to start your search at once, I suppose?" asked Bland.

"The sooner the better," said the other heartily.

"One moment."

It was the girl who spoke.

"You have a very good memory, señor?" she asked.

For just a fraction of a second the smile died from the man's eyes.

"I have an excellent memory, madame," he said curtly.

They went together in a cab and were admitted to Schiller's flat by the police officer on guard.

"Have you any theory?" asked Bland as they stood in the hall.

"Yes," replied the other quickly. "I think the documents are hidden in a recess in the wall behind a secret panel. It may take a week to find the panel. This is a very old house, and it is possible that Mr. Schiller chose it for some structural advantage it may have had."

Again Bland thought rapidly. The frankness of the man, his willingness to help, the talk of secret panels—all were in accordance with the girl's amazing prophecy.

He saw the glee in her eyes—glee at the mystification of her Chief.

Then he turned to the little man.

"Go ahead," he said.

Señor da Silva bowed.

"I will take this wall first," he said, "and I will search for the evidence of a panel. My fingers are perhaps more sensitive than yours—"

His hand was outstretched towards the dado, when—

"Stop!"

At the sound of the girl's sharp warning Señor da Silva turned.

"Before you go any farther," she said, "let me ask you if you value your life?"

The Chilian shrugged and spread his hands.

"Naturally, madame."

The girl turned to Bland.

"If this man learns Code 2, what will happen to him?"

Bland looked from Mary to the face of the stranger.

"He will certainly die," he said simply.

She nodded.

"You may go on if you wish, but you are starting a little too far to the right."

His face went a ghastly gray.

"To the right—!" he stammered.

"The message to you begins at the door, Señor Viztelli," she said calmly. "The code does not begin until you reach the window. Will you continue?"

He shook his head, having no words.

Bland called in his man, and they hustled the little South American into a cab.

"And now explain," said Bland.

The girl walked to the wall near the door and touched the dado.

"Feel," she said.

Bland's fingers touched the wallpaper gingerly. He felt a few pinpoint eruptions, passed his hand to the right, and felt more. Then the truth dawned on him.

"Braille!" he whispered.

The girl nodded.

"Schiller's father was a blind man," she said, "and Schiller evidently took up the study of the alphabet by which blind men read. Silva was informed how the code had been written and learned it against the time when it would be necessary to take over Schiller's work."

She ran her fingers along the dado.

"There are seven lines of writing, and they run around the room," she said. "Schiller pasted this dado on himself—a bit at a time—as fast as he was able to photograph Code 2. This is how the top line begins.

"To Raymond Viztelli," she read. "Keep up pretense of helping police; be frank, as I have told you. Tell them there is a secret panel, and you will be able to come often. Code Begins: Abraham means 'New guns have been fitted—'"

Bland caught her hand and gently drew it away.

"If you want to be a nice live girl and dine with me tonight," he said half humorously, "do not pursue your investigations any farther."

That afternoon Bland did a little amateur paper-stripping and made a good job of it.

The Problem Solver and the Spy

Christopher Anvil

Richard Verner leaned back in his office chair with the alert look of a big cat as, across the desk, Nathan Bancroft, a quietly dressed man of average height, spoke earnestly.

"Last Saturday, Mr. Verner, a technician at one of our most highly classified research laboratories got away with the plans for a new and secret type of laser device. The scientist who invented the device evidently tried to stop him, and was stabbed to death."

Verner nodded intently.

Bancroft went on. "To understand the situation that's come about, you have to know that the region around this laboratory has a great many caverns. These are connected in a gigantic system of natural tunnels, rooms, crevices, and underground streams that have never been thoroughly mapped or explored.

"The technologist who stole the plans is an ardent speleologist—cave explorer. Possibly one reason for his hobby is that he suffers from hay fever, and cavern air is pure. In any case, over a period of years he's spent entire days in an underground complex of branching tunnels known as the Maze of Minos. A number of cave explorers have been lost in there, and the local people shun it. The only known expert on this underground maze is the murderer himself.

"Now there's no question, Mr. Verner, but that this spy expected to be far away before the theft of the plans was discovered. But, by sheer good luck, the director of the laboratory discovered what had happened and immediately notified the police. The police were lucky too—they spotted the technician's car just after the call came in. But then we all ran out of luck. The technician, taking the plans with him, escaped into this cavern—this Maze of Minos."

"And got away?" said Verner.

"Got clean away," said Bancroft. "The tunnels branch off in all directions, and of course it's as dark in there as the blackest possible night. He simply vanished."

Verner nodded again. "He's still in there?"

Bancroft said glumly, "Yes, he's still in there. We have a great many men on the spot, doing nothing but watching the known exits. But there's always the chance that he'll find some new way out, or knows of one, and get away. Meanwhile, we desperately need those plans. With the inventor dead, there are certain details we can clear up only from those papers. Yet, if we should get close, he just might take it into his head to destroy them. What we want to do is get to him before he realizes we're near. But how? How do we even *find* him in there?"

"Is he starving?"

"Not likely. He probably has caches of food for his longer explorations. And there's water in the caverns, if you know where to look."

"You want to get him alive, and by surprise?"

"Exactly."

"But he knows you're hunting for him in the cavern?"

"Oh, yes. We've brought in lights, and before we realized what we were up against, we set up loudspeakers and warned him to give up, or we'd come in after him. If he understood what we were saying over all the echoes, this must have amused him immensely. We could put our whole organization in there and get nothing out of a grand-scale search but sore feet, chills, and a dozen men lost in the winding passages. The thing is a standoff, and he knows it."

Verner asked thoughtfully, "And what brings you to me?"

Bancroft smiled. "We've consulted cave explorers, geologists, and all kinds of specialists without finding what we want. Then one of our men, who knows General Granger, remembered his saying he'd been helped in that mess at the hunting lodge by a 'heuristician.' We got in touch with Granger, who recommended you highly. We didn't know exactly what a 'heuristician' was—but we're prepared to try anything."

Verner laughed. "A heuristician is a professional problem solver. I work on the assumption that nearly all problems can be solved by the same basic technique, combined with expert knowledge. Some of my cases are scientific, some involve business situations, and others are purely personal problems. The details vary, but the basic technique remains the same. If the case interests me enough to take it in the first place, and if the necessary expert help is available, I can usually solve any problem—though sometimes there's an unavoidable element of luck and uncertainty."

"Well," said Bancroft, "we have plenty of experts on hand—all kinds. And I hope this problem offers enough of a challenge to interest you."

Verner nodded. "And we'd better lose no time getting there."

Many cars and several big trucks were parked outside the main cavern entrance. From outside, electric cables coiled into the brilliantly lighted mouth of the cavern, and there was a steady throb of engines as Verner and Bancroft walked in.

"Generators," said Bancroft. "We're trying to light this end as brightly as possible, and extend the lights inward. But it's a hopeless job. I'll show you why."

They pushed past a crowd of men, who nodded to Bancroft and glanced at Verner curiously. Then they were in a brightly lighted chamber in the rock, about forty feet long by ten high, and twelve to fourteen feet wide. Here their voices and footsteps echoed as Bancroft led the way toward the far end, where a faint breeze of cool air blew in their faces.

"So far, so good," said Bancroft, stepping around a tangle of cables and walking through a narrow doorway cut in the rock. "But here we begin to run into trouble."

He stepped back to show a long brightly lit chamber where fantastic frieze-like shapes dipped from the ceiling to meet fairy castles and miniature ranges of mountains rising from the floor. Here the electric cables that lay along the floor fanned out in all directions, to wind around huge pointed cones into the well-lighted distance.

Wherever Verner looked, the stalactites and stalagmites rose and dipped endlessly, with new chambers opening out in different directions, and as Bancroft led the way, they clambered over the uneven slanting floor past waterfalls of rock, through little grottoes, and by shapes like thrones, statues, and weird creatures from fairyland.

For a long time they walked in silence except for the echoes of their own footsteps. Then suddenly it was dark ahead. The last giant electric bulb lit the shapes of stalagmites rising one behind the other, till the farthest ones were lost in impenetrable shadows.

A gentle breeze was still in their faces—cool, refreshing, and pure. Somewhere ahead they could hear a faint trickling of water.

"Here," said Bancroft, "we come to the end of our string. These tunnels branch, then open out into rooms, and the rooms have galleries leading off from them, and out of these galleries there are still more tunnels. They twist, wind, and occasionally they even rejoin."

His voice echoed as he talked, and he pointed off to the right. "Over there, somewhere—I think that's the direction—there's an eighty-foot sheer drop with a little stream at the bottom, and from the wall of this drop other tunnels open out in various directions and on different levels. There are eyeless fish in the stream, and a kind of blind salamander—very interesting, but our problem is the complex of all those tunnels. A man who knew where he was going could pick the one tunnel he wanted out of a dozen or so at any given place. But we have to follow them all. And every so often they divide again or—look up there."

Bancroft pointed to a dark opening above a slope like a frozen waterfall.

"Probably that's another one. This whole place is honeycombed, filled with diverging and connecting tunnels. It's like trying to track down someone inside a man-size termite's nest. We thought he might have left some trace, some sign of where he'd gone. We thought we could follow him with dogs. We forgot that he's practically lived in here during his spare time ever since the laboratory was set up.

"There's a superabundance of clues. Dogs have followed one track through the dark right over the edge of a sudden drop, and been killed. We can find signs that he's been just about anywhere we look. We found a pair of sneakers at one place, and a cache of food at another." Bancroft shook his head. "Let's go out. There are some people you'll want to meet, now that you've seen what it's like in here, what our problem is."

* / * * * *

Outside, in the warm fall night, a group of men quickly gathered around Verner and Bancroft.

One, an old man in dungarees and checked shirt, was well known locally as a cave explorer. A tall man in a gray business suit was the director of the government laboratory, and he repeatedly sneezed and blew his nose. A boy in dungarees and old leather jacket told how he had seen the murderer-spy enter the cave, after crossing a nearby field; he was sure it was the man they were looking for.

"Heck, we all knew him. We'd often see him go in here. He knows more about these caves than anyone—well, except maybe Gramps Peters here."

The old man laughed. "Don't fool yourself. I know old Minotaur, at the other end of this, like I know the back of my hand. But this Maze—I admit I don't know it. I was in here maybe ten years ago, got lost, wandered around for five days, drinking the water in an underground stream, and finally made my way out of a collapsed sinkhole miles away from here. That was the end of the Maze for me. Now, this man you're looking for is a different animal. He's as good as lived in there."

The laboratory director sneezed and blew his nose again. "One reason he spent so much time there, especially in the fall, was the pure air of the caverns. He was, if anything, even more allergic than I am. He once told me that the only place an active man could find recreation out of doors in the fall, if he suffered from hay fever, was inside a cave."

Bancroft said, "We're watching all the known exits. We've sent teams of men through those tunnels, and we've only begun to grasp the difficulties. Somehow we've *got* to locate him—but how?"

Verner glanced at the old man. "There seems to be a slight steady current of air in there. That doesn't come from the outside, does it?"

"Gramps" Peters shook his head. "These passages are complicated, but in this part of the cavern most of the passages slope a little uphill. Up at the other end is what they call the Minotaur. There's an underground riverbed there; no river—that's eaten its way farther down—but there's this gentle flow of cold air. I suppose the air comes from the outside somewhere, maybe from hundreds of miles away, but you wouldn't know it by the time it gets here. It seems to flow into the Minotaur, and then branch out through the Maze. It's always fresh and cool. If you get turned around in a passage, that gentle breeze, when you come to a narrow place, will tell you which way you're headed."

When Verner was finished asking questions, Bancroft took him aside.

"You see now what we're up against, Mr. Verner?"

"I suppose you've got infrared equipment?"

"Yes, and if we knew where he was, it might help us find our way to him in the dark without warning him. But it won't help to send teams of men prospecting at random through all those tunnels. The last time we tried it we found nothing and three men were seriously injured when they came to a sudden slope." He looked at Verner tensely. "Do you have *any* suggestion, any idea at all?"

Verner nodded. "If we're lucky, and if what we've been told is true, we *may* have him out of there in a few hours."

"If you can do that, you're a miracle worker."

"No miracle at all—just common sense. But this is a case where we'll need a little luck. And we'll have to work from the upper end—from the Minotaur."

The passages of the Minotaur were larger and looked less complicated than those in the Maze. Here the gentle current of cool air seemed stronger, steadier, and could sometimes be felt even in comparatively wide passages.

Verner and Bancroft waited tensely, and then down the passage ahead came a small group, carrying a struggling man who was swearing violently.

"*Find* him?" said one of his captors, grinning. "All we had to do was follow the sounds he was making. He was sitting by a cache of food that would have lasted a week, with the plans still in his pocket."

Bancroft was looking at Verner, but he didn't speak. An awful choking and strangling from the prisoner made Bancroft turn in amazement. The choking and strangling noises were interspersed with violent sneezing.

Down the passage the men had stopped thrashing the stacks of ragweed ordered by Verner, which had sent thick clouds of pollen drifting through the passage and into the Maze. The pollen had unerringly found its target—the murderer-thief who suffered from hay fever.

The Uninvited

Michael Gilbert

Mr. Calder was silent, solitary and generous with everything, from a basket of cherries or mushrooms, to efficient first aid to a child who had tumbled. The children liked him. But their admiration was reserved for his dog.

The great, solemn, sagacious Rasselas was a deerhound. He had been born in the sunlight. His coat was the color of dry sherry, his nose was blue-black and his eyes shone like worked amber. From the neat tufts at his heels to the top of his dome-shaped head, there was a royalty about him. He had lived in courts and consorted on his own terms with other princes.

Mr. Calder's cottage stood at the top of a fold in the Kentish Downs. The road curled up to it from Lamperdown, in the valley. First it climbed slowly between woods, then forked sharply left and rose steeply, coming out onto the plateau, rounded and clear as a bald pate. The road served only the cottage, and stopped in front of its gate.

Beyond the house, there were paths which led

through the home fields and into the woods beyond, woods full of primroses, bluebells, pheasants' eggs, chestnuts, hollow trees and ghosts. The
woods did not belong to Mr. Calder. They belonged, in theory, to a syndicate of business men
from the Medway towns, who came at the weekends, in autumn and winter, to kill birds. When
the sound of their shooting brakes announced
their arrival, Mr. Calder would call Rasselas indoors. At all other times, the great dog roamed
freely in the garden and in the three open fields
which formed Mr. Calder's domain. But he never
went out of sight of the house, nor beyond the
sound of his master's voice.

The children said that the dog talked to the
man, and this was perhaps not far from the truth.
Before Mr. Calder came, the cottage had been
inhabited by a bad-tempered oaf who had looked
on himself as custodian for the Medway sportsmen, and had chased and harried the children
who, in their turn, had become adept at avoiding
him.

When Mr. Calder first came, they had spent a
little time in trying him, before finding him
harmless. Nor had it taken them long to find out
something else. No one could cross the plateau
unobserved, small though he might be and quietly
though he might move. A pair of sensitive ears
would have heard, a pair of amber eyes would have
seen; and Rasselas would pad in at the open door
and look inquiringly at Mr. Calder who would say,
"Yes, it's the Lightfoot boys and their sister. I saw
them, too." And Rasselas would stalk out and lie

down again in his favorite day bed, on the sheltered side of the woodpile.

Apart from the children, visitors to the cottage were a rarity. The postman wheeled his bicycle up the hill once a day; delivery vans appeared at their appointed times; the fish man on Tuesdays, the grocer on Thursdays, the butcher on Fridays. In the summer, occasional hikers wandered past, unaware that their approach, their passing and their withdrawal had all been reported to the owner of the cottage.

Mr. Calder's only regular visitor was Mr. Behrens, the retired schoolmaster, who lived in the neck of the valley, two hundred yards outside Lamperdown Village, in a house which had once been the Rectory. Mr. Behrens kept bees, and lived with his aunt. His forward-stooping head, his wrinkled, brown skin, blinking eyes and cross expression made him look like a tortoise which has been roused untimely from its winter sleep.

Once or twice a week, summer and winter, Mr. Behrens would get out his curious tweed hat and his iron-tipped walking stick, and would go tip-tapping up the hill to have tea with Mr. Calder. The dog knew and tolerated Mr. Behrens, who would scratch his ears and say, "Rasselas. Silly name. *You* came from Persia, not Abyssinia." It was believed that the two old gentlemen played backgammon.

There were other peculiarities about Mr. Calder's menage which were not quite so very apparent to the casual onlooker.

When he first took over the house, some of the

alterations he had asked for had caused Mr. Benskin, the builder, to scratch his head. Why, for instance, had he wanted one perfectly good southern-facing window filled in, and two more opened, on the north side of the house?

Mr. Calder had been vague. He said that he liked an all-round view and plenty of fresh air. In which case, asked Mr. Benskin, why had he insisted on heavy shutters on all downstairs windows and a steel plate behind the woodwork of the front and back doors?

There had also been the curious matter of the telephone line. When Mr. Calder had mentioned that he was having the telephone installed, Mr. Benskin had laughed. The post office, over-whelmed as they were with post-war work, were hardly likely to carry their line of poles a full mile up the hill for one solitary cottage. But Mr. Benskin had been wrong, and on two counts. Not only had the post office installed a telephone, with surprising promptness, but they had actually dug a trench and brought it in underground.

When this was reported to him, Mr. Benskin had told the public ear of the Golden Lion that he had always known there was something odd about Mr. Calder.

"He's an inventor," he said. "To my mind, there's no doubt that's what he is. An inventor. He's got government support. Otherwise, how'd he get a telephone line laid like that?"

Had Mr. Benskin been able to observe Mr. Calder getting out of bed in the morning, he would have been fortified in his opinion. For it is a well-known fact that inventors are odd, and Mr. Calder's routine on rising was very odd indeed.

Summer and winter, he would wake half an hour before dawn. He turned on no electric light. Instead, armed with a big torch, he would pad downstairs, the cold nose of Rasselas a few inches behind him, and make a minute inspection of the three ground-floor rooms. On the edges of the shutters were certain tiny, thread-like wires, almost invisible to the naked eye. When he had satisfied himself that these were in order, Mr. Calder would return upstairs and get dressed.

By this time, day was coming up. The darkness had withdrawn across the bare meadows and chased the ghosts back into the surrounding woods. Mr. Calder would take a pair of heavy naval binoculars from his dressing table, and, sitting back from the window, would study with care the edges of his domain. The inspection was repeated from the window on the opposite side.

Then, whistling softly to himself, Mr. Calder would walk downstairs to cook breakfast for himself and for Rasselas.

The postman, who arrived at eleven o'clock, brought the newspapers with the letters. Perhaps because he lived alone and saw so few people, Mr. Calder seemed particularly fond of his letters and papers. He opened them with a loving care which an observer might have found ludicrous. His fingers caressed the envelope, or the wrapping paper, very gently, as a man will squeeze a cigar. Often he would hold an envelope up to the light as if he could read, through the outer covering, the message inside. Sometimes, he would even weigh an envelope in the delicate letter scales which he kept on top of his desk between a stuffed seagull and a night-scented jasmine in a pot.

On a fine morning in May, when the sun was fulfilling, in majesty, the promise of a misty dawn, Mr. Calder unfolded his copy of the *Times*, turned, as was his custom, to the foreign news pages, and started to read.

He had stretched his hand out toward his coffee cup when he stopped. It was a tiny check, a break in the natural sequence of his actions, but it was enough to make Rasselas look up. Mr. Calder smiled reassuringly at the dog. His hand resumed its movement, picked up the cup, carried it to his mouth. But the dog was not easy.

Mr. Calder read, once more, the five-line item which had caught his attention. Then he glanced at his watch, went across to the telephone, dialed a Lamperdown number and spoke to Jack at the garage, which also ran a taxi service.

"Just do it if we hurry," said Jack. "No time to spare. I'll come right up."

While he waited for the taxi, Mr. Calder first telephoned Mr. Behrens to warn him that they might have to postpone their game of backgammon. Then he spent a little time telling Rasselas that he was leaving him in charge of the cottage, but that he would be back before dark. Rasselas swept the carpet with his feathery tail, and made no attempt to follow Mr. Calder when Jack's

Austin came charging up the hill and reversed in front of the cottage gate.

In the end, the train was ten minutes late at the junction, and Mr. Calder caught it with ease.

He got out at Victoria, walked down Victoria Street, turned to the right, opposite the open space where the Colonial Office used to stand, and to the right again into the Square. In the southwest corner stands the Westminster branch of the London and Home Counties Bank.

Mr. Calder walked into the bank. The head cashier, Mr. Macleod, nodded gravely to him and said, "Mr. Fortescue is ready. You can go straight in."

"I'm afraid the train was late," said Mr. Calder. "We lost ten minutes at the junction, and never caught it up."

"Trains are not as reliable now as they used to be," agreed Mr. Macleod.

A young lady from a nearby office had just finished banking the previous day's takings. Mr. Macleod was watching her out of the corner of his eye until the door had shut behind her. Then he said, with exactly the same inflection, but more softly, "Will it be necessary to make any special arrangements for your departure?"

"Oh, no, thank you," said Mr. Calder. "I took all the necessary precautions."

"Fine," said Mr. Macleod.

He held open the heavy door, paneled in sham walnut in the style affected by pre-war bank designers, ushered Mr. Calder into the anteroom and left him there for a few moments.

Then the head cashier reappeared and held open the door for Mr. Calder.

Mr. Fortescue, who came forward to greet him, would have been identified in any company as a bank manager. It was not only the conventional dress, the square, sagacious face, the suggestion that as soon as his office door closed behind him, he would extract an old pipe and push it into his discreet but friendly mouth. It was more than that. It was the bearing, the balance, the air of certainty and stability which sits upon a man when he is the representative of a corporation with a hundred million pounds of disclosed assets.

"Nice to see you," he said. "Grab a chair. Any trouble on the way up?"

"No trouble," said Mr. Calder. "I don't think anything can start for another two or three weeks."

"They might have post-dated the item to put you off your guard." He picked up his own copy of the *Times* and re-read the four and a half lines of print which recorded that Colonel Josef Weinleben, the international expert on bacterial antibodies, had died in Klagenfurt as the result of an abdominal operation.

"No," said Calder. "He wanted me to read it, and sweat."

"It would be the established procedure to organize his own 'death' before setting on a serious mission," Mr. Fortescue agreed. He picked up a heavy paper knife and tapped thoughtfully with it on the desk. "But it could be true, this time.

Weinleben must be nearly sixty."

"He's coming," said Mr. Calder. "I can feel it in my bones. It may even be true that he's ill. If he was dying, he'd like to take me along with him."

"What makes you so sure?"

"I tortured him," said Mr. Calder. "And broke him. He'd never forget."

"No," said Mr. Fortescue. He held the point of the paper knife toward the window, sighting down it as if it had been a pistol. "No. I think very likely you're right. We'll try to pick him up at the port, and tag him. But we can't guarantee to stop him getting in. If he tries to operate, of course, he'll have to show his hand. You've got your permanent cover. Do you want anything extra?"

He might, thought Mr. Calder, have been speaking to a customer. You've got your normal overdraft. Do you want any extra accommodation, Mr. Calder? The bank is here to serve you. There was something at the same time ridiculous and comforting in treating life and death as though they were entries in the same balance sheet.

"I'm not at all sure that I want you to stop him," he said. "We aren't at war. You could only deport him. It might be more satisfactory to let him through."

"Do you know," said Mr. Fortescue, "the same thought had occurred to me."

Mrs. Farmer, who kept the Seven Gables Guest House, between Aylesford and Bearsted, considered Mr. Wendon a perfect guest. His passport and the card which he had duly filled in on arrival showed him to be a Dutchman; but his English, though accented in odd places, was colloquial and fluent. An upright, red-faced, gray-haired man, he was particularly nice with Mrs. Farmer's two young children. Moreover, he gave no trouble. He was—and this was a sovereign virtue in Mrs. Farmer's eyes—methodical and predictable.

Every morning, in the endless succession of fine days which heralded that summer, he would go out walking, clad in aged but respectable tweed, field glasses over one shoulder, a small knapsack on the other for camera, sandwiches and thermos flask. And in the evenings, he would sit in the lounge, entertaining Tom and Rebecca with accounts of the birds he had observed that day. It was difficult to imagine, seeing him sitting there, gentle, placid and upright, that he had killed men and women—and children, too—with his own well-kept hands. But then Mr. Wendon, or Weinleben, or Weber, was a remarkable man.

On the tenth day of his stay, he received a letter from Holland. Its contents seemed to cause him some satisfaction, and he read it twice before putting it away in his wallet. The stamps he tore off, giving them to Mrs. Farmer for Tom.

"I may be a little late this evening," he said. "I am meeting a friend at Maidstone. Don't keep dinner for me."

That morning, he packed his knapsack with particular care and caught the Maidstone bus at Aylesford crossroads. He had said that he was going to Maidstone and he never told unnecessary lies.

After that, his movements became somewhat complicated, but by four o'clock, he was safely ensconced in a dry ditch to the north of the old Rectory at Lamperdown. Here he consumed a biscuit, and observed the front drive of the house.

At a quarter past four, Jack arrived with his taxi and Mr. Behrens' aunt came out, wearing, despite the heat of the day, coat and gloves and a rather saucy scarf, and was installed in the back seat. Mr. Behrens handed in her shopping basket, waved good-by and retired into the house.

Five minutes later, Mr. Wendon was knocking at the front door. Mr. Behrens opened it, and blinked when he saw the gun in his visitor's hand.

"I must ask you to turn around and walk in front of me," said Mr. Wendon.

"Why should I?" said Mr. Behrens. He sounded more irritated than alarmed.

"If you don't, I shall shoot you," said Mr. Wendon. He said it exactly as if he meant it and pushed Mr. Behrens toward a door.

After a moment, Mr. Behrens wheeled about, and asked, "Where now?"

"That looks the sort of place I had in mind," said Mr. Wendon. "Open the door and walk in. But quite slowly."

It was a small, dark room, devoted to hats, coats, sticks, old tennis rackets, croquet mallets, bee veils and such.

"Excellent," said Mr. Wendon. He helped himself to the old-fashioned tweed hat and the iron-tipped walking stick which Mr. Behrens carried abroad with him on all his perambulations of the countryside. "A small window, and a stout, old door. What could be better?"

Still watching Mr. Behrens closely, he laid the hat and stick on the hall table, dipped his left hand into his own coat pocket and brought out a curious-looking metal object.

"You have not, perhaps, seen one of these before? It works on the same principle as a Mills grenade, but is six times as powerful and is incendiary as well as explosive. When I shut this door, I shall bolt it and hang the grenade from the upturned bolt. The least disturbance will dislodge it. It is powerful enough to blow the door down."

"All right," said Mr. Behrens. "But get on with it. My sister will be back soon."

"Not until eight o'clock, if she adheres to last week's arrangements," said Mr. Wendon quite knowingly.

He closed the door, shot the bolts, top and bottom, and suspended the grenade with artistic care from the top one.

Mr. Calder had finished his tea by five o'clock, and then shortly afterward strolled down to the end of the paddock, where he was repairing the fence. Rasselas lay quietly in the lee of the wood pile. The golden afternoon turned imperceptibly toward evening.

Rasselas wrinkled his velvet muzzle to dislodge a fly. On one side, he could hear Mr. Calder digging with his mattock into the hilltop chalk and grunting as he dug. Behind, some four fields away, a horse, fly-plagued, was kicking its heels and bucking. Then, away to his left, he located a familiar sound. The clink of an iron-tipped walking stick on the stone.

Rasselas liked to greet the arrival of this particular friend of his master, but he waited, with dignity, until the familiar tweed had come into view. Then he unfolded himself and trotted gently out into the road.

So strong was the force of custom, so disarming were the familiar and expected sight and sound, that even Rasselas' five senses were lulled. But his instinct was awake. The figure was still a dozen paces off and advancing confidently, when Rasselas stopped. His eyes searched the figure. Right appearance, right hat, right noises. But wrong gait. Quicker, and more purposeful than their old friend. And, above all, wrong smell.

The dog hackled, then crouched as if to jump. But it was the man who jumped. He leaped straight at the dog, his hand came out from under his coat and the loaded stick hissed through the air with brutal force. Rasselas was still moving and the blow missed his head, but struck him full on the back of the neck. He went down without a sound.

Mr. Calder finished digging the socket for the corner post he was planting, straightened his back and decided that he would fetch the brush and creosote from the house. As he came out of the paddock, he saw the great dog lying in the road.

He ran forward and knelt in the dust. There was no need to look twice.

He hardly troubled to raise his eyes when a

voice which he recognized spoke from behind him.

"Keep your hands in sight," said Colonel Weinleben, "and try not to make any sudden or unexpected move."

Mr. Calder got up.

"I suggest we move back into the house," said the colonel. "We shall be more private there. I should like to devote at least as much attention to you as you did to me on the last occasion we met."

Mr. Calder seemed hardly to be listening. He was looking down at the crumpled, empty, tawny skin, incredibly changed by the triviality of life's departure. His eyes were full of tears.

"You killed him," he said.

"As I shall shortly kill you," said the colonel. And as he spoke, he spun round like a startled marionette, took a stiff pace forward and fell, face downward.

Mr. Calder looked at him incuriously. From the shattered hole in the side of his head, dark blood ran out and mixed with the white dust. Rasselas had not bled at all. He was glad of that tiny distinction between the two deaths.

It was Mr. Behrens who had killed Colonel Weinleben, with a single shot from a .312 rifle, fired from the edge of the wood. The rifle was fitted with a telescopic sight, but the shot was a fine one, even for an excellent marksman such as Mr. Behrens.

He'd run for nearly a quarter of a mile before firing it; he had to get into position very quickly, and he had only just been able to see the colonel's head over the top of an intervening hedge.

He burst through this hedge now, saw Rasselas and started to curse.

"It wasn't your fault," said Mr. Calder. He was sitting in the road, the dog's head in his lap.

"If I'm meant to look after you, I ought to look after you properly," said Mr. Behrens. "Not let myself be jumped by an amateur like that. I hadn't reckoned on him blocking the door with a grenade. I had to break out of the window, and it took me nearly half an hour."

"We've a lot to do," said Mr. Calder. He got stiffly to his feet and went to fetch a spade.

Between them they dug a deep grave, behind the wood pile, and laid the dog in it, and filled it in, and patted the earth into a mound. It was a fine resting place, looking out southward over the feathery tops of the trees, across the Weald of Kent. A resting place for a prince.

Colonel Weinleben they buried later, with a good deal more haste and less ceremony, in the wood. He was greatly inferior to the dog, both in birth and breeding.

QL696.C9

Anthony Boucher

The librarian's body had been removed from the swivel chair, but Detective Lieutenant Donald MacDonald stood beside the desk. This was only his second murder case, and he was not yet hardened enough to use the seat freshly vacated by a corpse. He stood and faced the four individuals, one of whom was a murderer.

"Our routine has been completed," he said, "and I've taken a statement from each of you. But before I hand in my report, I want to go over those statements in the presence of all of you. If anything doesn't jibe, I want you to say so."

The librarian's office of the Serafin Pelayo branch of the Los Angeles Public Library was a small room. The three witnesses and the murderer (but which was which?) sat crowded together. The girl in the gray dress—Stella Swift, junior librarian—shifted restlessly. "It was all so . . . so confusing and so awful," she said.

MacDonald nodded sympathetically. "I know." It was this girl who had found the body. Her eyes were dry now, but her nerves were still tense. "I'm sorry to insist on this, but . . ." His glance surveyed the other three: Mrs. Cora Jarvis, children's librarian, a fluffy kitten; James Stickney, library patron, a youngish man with no tie and wild hair; Norbert Utter, high-school teacher, a lean, almost ascetic-looking man of forty-odd. One of these . . .

"Immediately before the murder," MacDonald began, "the branch librarian Miss Benson was alone in the office typing. Apparently" (he gestured at the sheet of paper in the typewriter) "a draft for a list of needed replacements. This office can be reached only through those stacks, which can in turn be reached only by passing the main desk. Mrs. Jarvis, you were then on duty at that desk, and according to you only these three people were then in the stacks. None of them, separated as they were in the stacks, could see each other or the door of this office." He paused.

The thin teacher spoke up. "But this is ridiculous, officer. Simply because I was browsing in the stacks to find some fresh ideas for outside reading . . ."

The fuzzy-haired Stickney answered him. "The Loot's right. Put our stories together, and it's got to be one of us. Take your medicine, comrade."

"Thank you, Mr. Stickney. That's the sensible attitude. Now Miss Benson was shot, to judge by position and angle, from that doorway. The weapon was dropped on the spot. All four of you claim to have heard that shot from your respective locations and hurried toward it. It was Miss Swift who opened the door and discovered the body. Understandably enough, she fainted. Mrs. Jarvis looked after her while Mr. Stickney had presence of mind enough to phone the police. All of you watched each other, and no one entered this room until our arrival. Is all that correct?"

Little Mrs. Jarvis nodded. "My, Lieutenant, you put it all so neatly! You should have been a cataloguer like Miss Benson."

"A cataloguer? But she was head of the branch, wasn't she?"

"She had the soul of a cataloguer," said Mrs. Jarvis darkly.

"Now this list that she was typing when she was killed." MacDonald took the paper from the typewriter. "I want you each to look at that and tell me if the last item means anything to you."

The end of the list read:

Davies: MISSION TO MOSCOW (2 cop)
Kernan: DEFENSE WILL NOT WIN THE WAR
FIC
MacInnes: ABOVE SUSP
QL696.C9

The paper went from hand to hand. It evoked nothing but frowns and puzzled headshakings.

"All right." MacDonald picked up the telephone pad from the desk. "Now can any of you tell me why a librarian should have jotted down the phone number of the F.B.I.?"

This question fetched a definite reaction from Stickney, a sort of wry exasperation; but it was

Miss Swift who answered, and oddly enough with a laugh. "Dear Miss Benson . . ." she said. "Of course she'd have the F.B.I.'s number. Professional necessity."

"I'm afraid I don't follow that."

"Some librarians have been advancing the theory, you see, that a librarian can best help defense work by watching what people use which books. For instance, if somebody keeps borrowing every work you have on high explosives, you know he's a dangerous saboteur planning to blow up the aqueduct and you turn him over to the G-men."

"Seriously? It sounds like nonsense."

"I don't know, Lieutenant. Aside from card catalogues and bird-study, there was one thing Miss Benson loved. And that was America. She didn't think it was nonsense."

"I see . . . And none of you has anything further to add to this story?"

"I," Mr. Utter announced, "have fifty themes to correct this evening and . . ."

Lieutenant MacDonald shrugged. "O.K. Go ahead. All of you. And remember you're apt to be called back for further questioning at any moment."

"And the library?" Mrs. Jarvis asked. "I suppose I'm the ranking senior in charge now and I . . ."

"I spoke to the head of the Branches Department on the phone. She agrees with me that it's best to keep the branch closed until our investigation is over. But I'll ask you and Miss Swift to report as usual tomorrow; the head of Branches will be here then too, and we can confer further on any matters touching the library itself."

"And tomorrow I was supposed to have a story hour. Well at least," the children's librarian sighed, "I shan't have to learn a new story tonight."

Alone, Lieutenant MacDonald turned back to the desk. He set the pad down by the telephone and dialed the number which had caught his attention. It took time to reach the proper authority and establish his credentials, but he finally secured the promise of a full file on all information which Miss Alice Benson had turned over to the F.B.I.

"Do you think that's it?" a voice asked eagerly.

He turned. It was the junior librarian, the girl with the gray dress and the gold-brown hair. "Miss Swift!"

"I hated to sneak in on you, but I want to know. Miss Benson was an old dear and I . . . I found her and . . . Do you think that's it? That she really did find out something for the F.B.I. and because she did . . . ?"

"It seems likely," he said slowly. "According to all the evidence, she was on the best of terms with her staff. She had no money to speak of, and she was old for a crime-of-passion set-up. Utter and Stickney apparently knew her only casually as regular patrons of this branch. What have we left for a motive, unless it's this F.B.I. business?"

"We thought it was so funny. We used to rib her about being a G-woman. And now . . . Lieutenant, you've got to find out who killed her." The girl's lips set firmly and her eyes glowed.

MacDonald reached a decision. "Come on."

"Come? Where to?"

"I'm going to drive you home. But first we're going to stop off and see a man, and you're going to help me give him all the facts of this screwball case."

"Who? Your superior?"

MacDonald hesitated. "Yes," he said at last. "My superior."

He explained about Nick Noble as they drove. How Lieutenant Noble, a dozen years ago, had been the smartest problem-cracker in the department. How his captain had got into a sordid scandal and squeezed out, leaving the innocent Noble to take the rap. How his wife had needed a vital operation just then, and hadn't got it. How the widowed and disgraced man had sunk until . . .

"Nobody knows where he lives or what he lives on. All we know is that we can find him at a little joint on North Main. Somewhere in the back of his mind is a precision machine that sorts the screwiest facts into the one inevitable pattern. He's the court of last appeal on a case that's nuts, and God knows this one is. QL696.C9 . . . Screwball Division, L.A.P.D., the boys call him."

The girl shuddered a little as they entered the Chula Negra Café. It was not a choice spot for the élite. Not that it was a dive, either; just a counter and booths for the whole-hearted eating and drinking of the Los Angeles Mexicans.

MacDonald remembered which booth was Nick Noble's sanctum. The little man sat there, staring

into a half-empty glass of sherry, his skin dead
white and his features sharp and thin. His eyes
were of a blue so pale that the irises were almost
invisible.

"Hi!" said MacDonald. "Remember me?"

One thin blue-veined hand swatted at the sharp
nose. The pale eyes rested on the couple.
"MacDonald . . ." Nick Noble smiled faintly.
"Glad. Sit down." He glanced at Stella Swift.

MacDonald coughed. "Miss Swift, Mr. Noble.
Miss Swift and I have a story to tell you."

Nick Noble's eyes gleamed dimly. "Trouble?"

"Trouble. Want to hear it?"

Nick Noble swatted at his nose again. "Fly," he
explained to the girl. "Stays there." There was no
fly. He drained his glass of sherry. "Give."

MacDonald gave, much the same précis that he
had given to the group in the office. When he had
finished, Nick Noble sat silent. Then he stirred
slightly and said to the girl, "This woman. Benson. What was she like?"

"She was nice," said Stella. "But of course she
was a cataloguer."

"Cataloguer?"

"You're not a librarian. You wouldn't understand what that means. But I gather that when
people go to library school—I never did, I'm just a
junior—most of them suffer through cataloguing,
but a few turn out to be born cataloguers. Those
are a race apart. They know a little of everything,
all the systems of classification, Dewey, Library of
Congress, down to the last number, and just how
many spaces you indent each item on a typed card,

and all about bibliography, and they shudder in their souls if the least little thing is wrong. They have eyes like eagles and memories like elephants."

"With that equipment," said MacDonald, "she might really have spotted something for the F.B.I."

"Might," said Nick Noble. Then to the girl, "Hobbies?"

"Miss Benson's? Before the war she used to be a devoted birdwatcher, but lately she's been all wrapped up in trying to spot saboteurs instead."

"I'm pretty convinced," MacDonald contributed, "that that's our angle, screwy as it sounds. The F.B.I. lead may point out our man, and there's still hope from the lab reports on prints and the paraffin test."

"Tests," Nick Noble snorted. "All you do is teach criminals what not to do."

"But if those fail us, we've got a message from Miss Benson herself telling us who killed her. And that's what I want you to figure out." He handed over the paper from the typewriter. "It's pretty clear what happened. She was typing, looked up, and saw her murderer with a gun. If she wrote down his name, he might see it and destroy the paper. So she left this cryptic indication. It can't possibly be part of the list she was typing. Mrs. Jarvis and Miss Swift don't recognize it as library routine. And the word above breaks off in the middle. Those letters and figures are her dying words. Can you read them?"

Nick Noble's pallid lips moved faintly. "Q L six nine six point C nine." He leaned back in the booth and his eyes glazed over. "Names," he said.

"Names?"

"Names of four."

"Oh, Norbert Utter, the teacher; James Stickney, the nondescript; Mrs. Cora Jarvis, the children's librarian; and Miss Stella Swift here."

"So." Nick Noble's eyes came to life again. "Thanks, MacDonald. Nice problem. Give you proof tonight."

Stella Swift gasped. "Does that mean that he . . . ?"

MacDonald grinned. "You're grandstanding for the lady, Mr. Noble. You can't mean that you've solved that QL business like that?"

"Pencil," Nick Noble said.

Wonderingly, Lieutenant MacDonald handed one over. Nick Noble took a paper napkin, scrawled two words, folded it, and handed it to Stella. "Not now," he warned. "Keep it. Show it to him later. Grandstanding . . . ! Need more proof first. Get it soon. Let me know about tests. F.B.I."

MacDonald rose, frowning. "I'll let you know. But how you can . . ."

"Good-by, Mr. Noble. It's been so nice meeting you."

But Nick Noble appeared not to hear Stella's farewell. He was staring into his glass and not liking what he saw there.

* * * * *

Lieutenant MacDonald drew up before the girl's rooming house. "I may need a lot of help on the technique of librarianship in this case," he said. "I'll be seeing you soon."

"Thanks for the ride. And for taking me to that strange man. I'll never forget how . . . It seems—I don't know—uncanny, doesn't it?" A little tremor ran through her lithe body.

"You know, you aren't exactly what I'd expected a librarian to be. I've run into the wrong ones. I think of them as something with flat shirtwaists and glasses and a bun. Of course Mrs. Jarvis isn't either, but you . . ."

"I do wear glasses when I work," Stella confessed. "And you aren't exactly what I'd expected a policeman to be, or I shouldn't have kept them off all this time." She touched her free flowing hair. "And you should see me with a bun."

"That's a date. We'll start with dinner and—"

"Dinner!" she exclaimed. "Napkin!" She rummaged in her handbag. "I won't tell you what he said, that isn't fair, but just to check on—" She unfolded the paper napkin.

She did not say another word, despite all Mac-Donald's urging. She waved good-by in pantomime, and her eyes, as she watched him drive off, were wide with awe and terror.

Lieutenant MacDonald glared at the reports on the paraffin tests of his four suspects. All four negative. No sign that any one of them had recently used a firearm. Nick Noble was right; all you do is teach criminals what not to do. They learn about nitrite specks in the skin, so a handkerchief wrapped over the hand . . . The phone rang.

"Lafferty speaking. Los Angeles Field Office, F.B.I. You wanted the dope on this Alice Benson's reports?"

"Please."

"O.K. She did turn over to us a lot of stuff on a man who'd been reading nothing but codes and ciphers and sabotage methods and explosives and God knows what all. Sounded like a correspondence course for the complete Fifth Columnist. We check up on him, and he's a poor devil of a pulp writer. Sure he wanted to know how to be a spy and a saboteur; but just so's he could write about 'em. We gave him a thorough going over; he's in the clear."

"Name?"

"James Stickney."

"I know him," said MacDonald dryly. "And is that all?"

"We'll send you the file, but that's the gist of it. I gather the Benson woman had something else she wasn't ready to spill, but if it's as much help as that was . . . Keep an eye on that library, though. There's something going on."

"How so?"

"Three times in the past two months we've trailed suspects into that Serafin Pelayo branch, and not bookworms either. They didn't do anything there or contact anybody, but that's pretty high for coincidence in one small branch. Keep an eye open. And if you hit on anything, maybe we can work together."

"Thanks. I'll let you know." MacDonald hung up. So Stickney had been grilled by the F.B.I. on Miss Benson's information. Revenge for the indignity? A petty motive. And still . . . The phone rang again.

"Lieutenant MacDonald? This is Mrs. Jarvis. Remember me?"

"Yes indeed. You've thought of something more about—?"

"I certainly have. I think I've figured out what that QL thing means. At least I think I've figured how we can find out what it means. You see . . ." There was a heavy sound, a single harsh thud. Mrs. Jarvis groaned.

"Mrs. Jarvis! What's the matter? Has anything —"

"Elsie . . ." MacDonald heard her say faintly. Then the line was dead.

"Concussion," the police surgeon said. "She'll live. Not much doubt of that. But she won't talk for several days, and there's no telling how much she'll remember then."

"Elsie," said Lieutenant MacDonald. It sounded like an oath.

"We'll let you know as soon as she can see you. O.K., boys. Get along." Stella Swift trembled as the stretcher bearers moved off. "Poor Cora . . . When her husband comes home from Lockheed and finds . . . I was supposed to have dinner with them tonight and I come here and find you . . ."

Lieutenant MacDonald looked down grimly at the metal statue. "The poor devil's track trophy, and they use it to brain his wife . . . And what brings you here?" he demanded as the lean figure of Norbert Utter appeared in the doorway.

"I live across the street, Lieutenant," the teacher explained. "When I saw the cars here and the ambulance, why naturally I . . . Don't tell me there's been another . . . ?"

"Not quite. So you live across the street? Miss Swift, do you mind staying here to break the news to Mr. Jarvis? It'd come easier from you than from me. I want to step over to Mr. Utter's for a word with him."

Utter forced a smile. "Delighted to have you, Lieutenant."

The teacher's simple apartment was comfortably undistinguished. His own books, MacDonald noticed, were chosen with unerring taste; the library volumes on a table seemed incongruous.

"Make yourself at home, Lieutenant, as I have no doubt you will. Now what is it you wanted to talk to me about?"

"First, might I use your phone?"

"Certainly."

MacDonald dialed the Chula Negra. Utter left the room. A Mexican voice answered, and Mac-Donald sent its owner to fetch Nick Noble. As he waited, he idly picked up one of those incongruous library books. He picked it up carelessly and it fell open. A slip of paper, a bookmark perhaps, dropped from the fluttering pages. MacDonald noticed typed letters:

430945q57w7qoOoqd3 . . .

"Noble here."

"Good." His attention snapped away from the paper. "Listen." And he told the results of the tests and the information from the F.B.I. and ended with the attack on Mrs. Jarvis. Utter came to the door once, looked at MacDonald, at the book, and at the paper. "And so," MacDonald concluded, "we've got a last message again. 'Elsie . . .' "

" 'Elsie . . .' " Nick Noble's voice repeated thoughtfully.

"Any questions?"

"No. Phone me tomorrow morning. Later tonight, maybe. Tell you then."

MacDonald hung up frowning. That paper . . . Suddenly he had it. The good old typewriter code, so easy to write and to decipher. For each letter use the key above it. He'd run into such a cipher in a case recently; he should be able to work it in his head. He visualized a keyboard. The letters and figures shifted into

reportatusualplace . . .

Mr. Utter came back and his lean face essayed a host's smile. "Refreshments, Lieutenant."

"Thank you."

"And now we can— Or should you care for a cheese cracker?"

"Don't bother."

"No bother." He left the room. Lieutenant MacDonald looked at the cipher, then at the glasses. Deftly he switched them. Then he heard the slightest sound outside the door, a sigh of expectation confirmed, and faint footsteps moving off. MacDonald smiled and switched the glasses back again.

Mr. Utter returned with a bowl of cheese wafers and the decanter. "To the success of your investigations, Lieutenant." They raised their glasses. Mr. Utter took a cautious sip, then coolly emptied his glass out the window. "You outsmarted me, Lieutenant," he announced casually. "I had not expected you to be up to the double gambit. I underrated you, and apologize." He filled his own glass afresh from the decanter, and they drank.

"So we're dropping any pretense?" said Mac-Donald.

Mr. Utter shrugged. "You saw that paper. I was unpardonably careless. You are armed and I am not. Pretense would be foolish when you can so readily examine the rest of those books."

Lieutenant MacDonald's hand stayed near his shoulder holster. "It was a good enough scheme. Certain prearranged books were your vehicles. Any accidental patron finding the messages, or even the average librarian, would pay little attention. Anything winds up as a marker in a library book. A few would be lost, but the safety made up for that. You prepared the messages here at home, returned them in the books so that you weren't seen inserting them in public . . ."

"You reconstruct admirably, Lieutenant."

"And who collected them?"

"Frankly, I do not know. The plan was largely arranged so that no man could inform on another."

"But Miss Benson discovered it, and Miss Benson had to be removed."

Mr. Utter shook his head. "I do not expect you to believe me, Lieutenant. But I have no more knowledge of Miss Benson's death than you have."

"Come now, Utter. Surely your admitted activities are catamount to a confession of—"

"Is *catamount* quite the word you want, Lieutenant?"

"I don't know. My tongue's fuzzy. So's my mind. I don't know what's wrong . . ."

Mr. Utter smiled, slowly and with great pleasure, "Of course, Lieutenant. Did you really think I had underrated you? Naturally I drugged both glasses. Then whatever gambit you chose, I had merely to refill my own."

Lieutenant MacDonald ordered his hand to move toward the holster. His hand was not interested.

"Is there anything else," Mr. Utter asked gently, "which you should care to hear—while you can still hear anything?"

The room began a persistent circular joggling.

* * * * *

Nick Noble wiped his pale lips and walked into the main library. At the information desk in the rotunda he handed a slip of paper to the girl in charge. On it was penciled

QL696.C9

The girl looked up, puzzled. "I'm sorry, but—"
"Elsie," said Nick Noble hesitantly.
The girl's face cleared. "Oh. Of course. Well, you see, in this library we . . ."

The crash of the door helped to clear Lieutenant MacDonald's brain. The shot set up thundering waves that ripped through the drugwebs in his skull. The cold water on his head and later the hot coffee inside finished the job.

At last he lit a cigarette and felt approximately human. The big man with the moon face, he gathered, was Lafferty, F.B.I. The girl, he had known in the first instant, was Stella Swift.

". . . just winged him when he tried to get out the window," Lafferty was saying. "The doc'll probably want us to lay off the grilling till tomorrow. Then you'll have your murderer, Mac, grilled and on toast."

MacDonald put up a hand to keep the top of his head on. "There's two things puzzle me. A, how you got here?"

Lafferty nodded at the girl.

"I began remembering things," she said, "after you went off with Mr. Utter. Especially I remembered Miss Benson saying just yesterday how she had some more evidence for the F.B.I. and how amazed she was that some people could show such an *utter* lack of patriotism. Then she laughed and I wondered why and only just now I realized it was because she'd made an accidental pun. There were other things too, and so I—"

"We had a note from Miss Benson today," Lafferty added. "It hadn't reached me yet when I phoned you. It was vaguely promising, no names, but it tied in well enough with what Miss Swift told us to make us check. When we found the door locked and knew you were here . . ."

"Swell. And God knows I'm grateful to you both. But my other puzzle: Just now, when Utter confessed the details of the message scheme thinking I'd never live to tell them, he still denied any knowledge of the murder. I can't help wondering . . ."

When MacDonald got back to his office, he found a memo:

The Public Library says do you want a book from the Main sent out to the Serafin Pelayo branch tomorrow morning? A man named Noble made the request, gave you as authority. Please confirm.

MacDonald's head was dizzier than ever as he confirmed, wondering what he was confirming.

The Serafin Pelayo branch was not open to the public the next morning, but it was well occupied. Outside in the reading room there waited the bandaged Mr. Utter, with Moon Lafferty on guard;

the tousle-haired James Stickney, with a sergeant from Homicide; Hank Jarvis, eyes bleared from a sleepless night at his wife's bedside; and Miss Trumpeter, head of the Branches Department, impatiently awaiting the end of this interruption of her well-oiled branch routine.

Here in the office were Lieutenant MacDonald, Stella Swift, and Nick Noble. Today the girl wore a bright red dress with a zipper which emphasized the fullness of her bosom. Lieutenant MacDonald held the book which had been sent out from the Main.

"Easy," he was saying. "Elsie. Not a name. Letters. L. C. Miss Swift mentioned systems of classification. Library of Congress."

"Of course," Stella agreed. "We don't use it in the Los Angeles Library; it's too detailed for a public system. But you have to study it in library school; so naturally I didn't know it, being a junior, but Mrs. Jarvis spotted it and Miss Benson, poor dear, must have known it almost by heart."

MacDonald read the lettering on the spine of the book. "U.S. Library of Congress Classification Q: Science."

Stella Swift sighed. "Thank Heavens. I was afraid it might be English literature."

MacDonald smiled. "I wonder if your parents knew nothing of literary history or a great deal, to name you Stella Swift."

Nick Noble grunted. "Go on."

MacDonald opened the book and thumbed

through pages. "QL: Zoology. QL 600, Verte-brates. QL 696, Birds, systematic list (subdivisions, A-Z)."

"Birds?" Stella wondered. "It was her hobby of course, but . . ."

MacDonald's eye went on down the page:

> e.g., .A2, Accipitriformes (Eagles, hawks, etc.)
> .A3, Alciformes (Auks, puffins)
> Alectorides, *see* Gruiformes

"Wonderful names," he said. "If only we had a suspect named Gruiformes . . . Point C seven," he went on, "Coraciiformes, see also . . . Here we are: Point C nine, Cypseli . . ."

The book slipped from his hands. Stella Swift jerked down her zipper and produced the tiny pistol which had contributed to the fullness of her bosom. Nick Noble's fleshless white hand lashed out and seized her wrist. The pistol stopped half-way to her mouth, twisted down, and discharged at the floor. The bullet went through the volume of L. C. classification just over the line reading

> .C9, Cypseli (Swifts)

A sober and embittered Lieutenant MacDonald unfolded the paper napkin taken from the prisoner's handbag and read, in sprawling letters:

STELLA SWIFT

"Her confession's clear enough," he said. "A German mother, family in the Fatherland, pressure brought to bear. . . . She was the inventor of this library-message system and running it unknown even to those using it, like Utter. After her false guess with Stickney, Miss Benson hit the truth with St . . . the Swift woman. She had to be disposed of. Then that meant more, attacking Mrs. Jarvis when she guessed too much and sacrificing Utter, an insignificant subordinate, as a scapegoat to account for Miss Benson's further hints to the F.B.I. But how did you spot it, and right at the beginning of the case?"

"Pattern," said Nick Noble. "Had to fit." His sharp nose twitched, and he brushed the nonexistent fly off it. "Miss Benson was cataloguer. QL business had to be book number. Not system used here or recognized at once, but some system. Look at names: Cora Jarvis, James Stickney, Norbert Utter, Stella Swift. Swift only name could possibly have classifying number."

"But weren't you taking a terrible risk giving her that napkin? What happened to Mrs. Jarvis . . ."

Noble shook his head. "She was only one knew you'd consulted me. Attack me, show her hand. Too smart for that. Besides, used to taking risks, when I . . ." He left unfinished the reference to the days when he had been the best detective lieutenant in Los Angeles.

Legacy of Danger

Patricia McGerr

The car curved up the approach to Memorial Bridge and Selena braced herself against a stab of memory. At the bridge's other end stood the golden equestrian statue on its massive pedestal into which Simon was said to have crashed on Friday night. It was late, he was driving fast, he lost control. Death was instantaneous. That was the story that appeared in the newspapers, the one Selena told her family and friends. But to her the bridge was only part of a network of deception. Somewhere in Washington, in some dark street, her husband had been killed. And Selena knew that his death was not accidental.

Section Q in Security had handled everything—the smashing of the car, the report to the police and to the papers, even selection of the undertaker, one who would not betray the fact that the supposed auto victim's only wound came from a knife. And late that night the man from Q had come to tell her gently what had happened and why it could not be revealed as murder.

Press and public must not grow curious about the assignment that had led to Simon's death. She accepted the reality as she had, throughout their marriage, accepted the risk. She had learned in those eight years to live with fear. Now she must begin to live again—with nothing.

The fact was heavy with irony. For Selena had, since childhood, been signaled as a girl who had everything. In her debutante years reporters coined fresh adjectives to describe the beauty of a face that was like a classic Greek statue brought to sparkling life by a hint of joyful secrets in the deep-set dark eyes and an almost gamin smile. Even now, though sparkle and smile were dimmed, the delicacy of her features, the cool ivory of her skin accented by her widow's black, the luminosity of grief gave birth to a new, perhaps more haunting beauty.

She had spent the night and day following the funeral at her family's Virginia estate and now she was going home. Home without Simon. At last she was back in the small Georgetown house that had known all their life together. But she was not alone long. Soon after she switched on the lights Hugh Pierce was once more sitting in her living room.

The shock of his message on Friday night had numbed her past any feeling of surprise at the identity of the messenger. Later, she found it fantastic that this neighbor, this old family friend, this dilettante painter was actually Simon's contact in Section Q. Hugh and her brother Jeff had been at Harvard together, and she remembered the time that Jeff, sighting his classmate from her window, had exclaimed with disgust, "Poor old Hugh. Terrible the way he's gone to seed. I think what ruined him was that proper Bostonian trust fund. Just enough coming in each month to take away his ambition."

"He has talent," Selena defended. "I saw some sketches he made in Africa last spring. They were very fine."

"He can do a good portrait," Jeff conceded. "But he only accepts a commission when, as he puts it, a face inspires him. Most of the time he's too busy expressing himself with circles and squares and zigzag lines. Just look at him! Baggy pants, a shirt that looks as if he used it to wipe brushes, and that great hound on a leash. And that's a man who was *magna cum*."

Tonight he wore the same old trousers and paint-smeared shirt, and the dog was corralled in Selena's back garden. But the vague, almost sleepy expression was gone from his face and his eyes had an alertness, a steeled purpose that made it easier to believe him a strong link in the Security chain, the man from whom Simon got his orders.

"I'm sorry to disturb you so soon." He moved quickly past the amenities. "But we can't waste time. The job Simon was on was urgent and important."

"They were always important." Bitterness edged her voice. "Always urgent."

"That's true," he agreed. "There's a great deal at stake."

Our country's at stake, she thought. Perhaps the

world. Against that, what's one man's death? Or one woman's desolation? She blinked her eyes to squeeze back the tears, crushed down the surge of self-pity. "Of course. If there's anything I can tell you—"

"On Friday night you said that Simon had not intended to work that evening, that it was a decision he made after you arrived at the Embassy party. Are you sure of that?"

"Quite sure. Simon never talked about his work. I knew his real job was intelligence, that his magazine writing was just a cover. But that's all. He never told me what he was investigating or where it might take him. I learned to ask no questions and show no surprise."

"It has to be that way," Hugh said soberly.

"But my point is that, while Simon had to keep things from me, whatever he did tell me was true. When he made a plan with me, I could be sure he intended to carry it out. And on Friday before we went to the Embassy reception he suggested we go on from there to a little place that's a favorite of ours for dinner.

"After he'd parked the car and we were walking up the driveway and into the Embassy he was reminding me of an iced meringue that's a specialty of that restaurant. Then when we were barely inside—it couldn't have been five minutes later— he suddenly changed, said he had work to do and—and left me."

"So it appears that something happened after you entered the Embassy that made him form a new plan. That's why I'm here. I want you to tell me all you remember, whom you saw, what they said. It may give us a lead on why he went off like that."

"I'll do my best." She shaded her eyes. The Secretary of State, on his way up the stairs, had smiled and waved. She gave Simon her wrap and at the checkstand a man in Air Force uniform asked him to stop by for a talk the next time he was in the Pentagon. Then she heard her own name and turned to see Mrs. Clayton coming through the door.

"Jedediah," she was calling back to her husband who was still descending from their car. "Here are the Meads! Isn't that a treat?"

The Senator agreed and asked her to make up her mind when the chauffeur should come back.

"Now how can I know how long we'll stay till I see who's here?" she argued. "Oh very well, tell him an hour." The Senator relayed her instructions to the chauffeur, then came on to join his wife. He inquired about Selena's mother and enveloped her in his usual gallantries.

"I'm a good judge of horseflesh," he declared, "but I never guessed the leggy colt scuffing sand in my eyes at Newport would grow into the sexiest filly in town."

"Jedediah!" His wife's reaction was ritual. "You're embarrassing Selena."

"Of course, I am. I enjoy embarrassing Selena. She's the only young woman I know who can blush. Come along, children, let's go up and see what kind of buffet our foreign aid money is buying."

"Jedediah! What a thing to say! And to a report-er, too."

"Lucymae!" he mimicked roguishly. "How you talk! Simon's no keyhole columnist to be interest-ed in my little indiscretions. Right, my boy?"

"Absolutely, Senator. But I'm going to miss both the buffet and your indiscretions. I have to check some facts for an article that's past dead-line. I only stopped to deliver Selena."

"I don't like these cocktail crushes by myself." Selena carried it on. Rule No. 1: never show surprise. "But I thought I ought to come, since this was one of Daddy's posts."

"So it was," the Senator nodded. "Well, Simon, you're the loser. We'll take care of Selena."

"Thank you, sir." He put the check for her wrap in her hand and closed her fingers over it with a special pressure that was at once thanks for her quickness on cue and apology for spoiling their evening. It was also a last good-by.

She summarized the conversation for Hugh and concluded, "So you see, it was quite routine and conventional, nothing out of the ordinary."

"I see." He studied her face for a moment, reached a decision. "I broke a rule on Friday by coming here to tell you about Simon's murder, thus letting you know our connection. Now I'm going to break another and tell you about the job Simon was on. If those few minutes in the Embas-sy started him on a fresh trail we need to know, as quickly as possible, what it was. You may have the key. It could be hidden in a compliment, a joke, a remark that seems too trivial to remember. But if you know our problem, what Simon was looking for, it may come back to you. Briefly, there's a leak from a Senate subcommittee that's holding hearings—closed and top secret—on a new version of the 3211 Samos reconnaissance satellite. So far the early testimony has been general and the figures only tentative. Fortunately, we found out about the leak before anything went out that can endanger our defense.

"Now, we're holding back the witnesses who can describe equipment and capabilities. But we can't stall the Senators much longer."

"But if they know there's a leak—"

"Before we suggest there's a security risk at the Capitol, we need 100-per-cent proof. Besides, if we announce we know there's a leak, that will give the other side a chance to cover up. So we've got to plug the hole before we let it out that we know it exists."

"If it has to do with the Samos program," Selena said thoughtfully, "that Air Force man may have some connection. He was a stranger to me. I only know he had two stars."

"We can check that out. But don't put all your concentration on the Air Force. There's one thing you should know. Your friend Senator Clayton is chairman of that subcommittee."

He gave her a phone number through which he could be reached day or night and a short time later he let himself and his black Newfoundland out through the small gate into the alley that connected with his house at the other end of the block. But he hesitated a moment beside her in the doorway.

"What will you do now, Selena? Have you thought of carrying on Simon's work?"

"Yes," she answered. "I did a little writing before we were married. And I often helped Simon with his articles, especially when one of your assignments took him away in the middle of one."

"So you're accustomed to finishing Simon's jobs?"

"Yes," she said, "I am."

And there they both let the matter rest. But she knew he was not recommending that she take up magazine writing. Hugh had asked her to scrape her memory. If she could reconstruct those few minutes in the Embassy and recall the exact instant of his tensing, she might reach an answer. Perhaps seeing the Claytons again would bring the clue.

The next day she phoned Mrs. Clayton and, predictably, received an invitation to dine—"just the three of us, a little family meal"—that same evening. In late afternoon she went to the Senator's office to ride with him to his house in Chevy Chase.

"What comfort!" She sank back against the cushions of the sleek black limousine.

"Only had this one two months." He responded with the normal male pride in his machine.

"And how thick that glass is." She indicated the partition separating them from the driver's seat.

"Double strength," he beamed. "I had it set in solid and immovable so this section is completely soundproof at all times. Grumman can bless the other drivers without scorching my ears and I can talk to my friends in greater secrecy than in my own office. If you tell me any secrets, my dear, they'll be just between you and me and the laprobe."

"I'd like to have secrets with you." She smiled at him. "It would be like old times."

"When you were a little girl and I was your Uncle Jed." He patted her hand and in the process seemed to be admiring her lovely profile. "Lucymae and I are very pleased that you chose to come to us this evening."

"I practically invited myself," she admitted, "but I knew you wouldn't mind. Oh!" She caught her breath. "I just remembered—I've had trouble sleeping and I was to get some tablets. The prescription's at a drugstore at the corner of Wisconsin and O Street. Would it be much trouble to stop there?"

"Of course we'll stop." He reached behind him to flip a switch under a small screen set into the back of the seat between them. "It gives me a chance to demonstrate my chatterbox. Grumman, there's a change in flight plan. We'll make a stop at—what's the address, my dear?"

"1300 Wisconsin Avenue."

"Got that, Grumman? Fine."

The man touched his cap in acknowledgment and the Senator pushed the switch into off position. For the next few minutes she was glad to let him do the talking, while within her suspense and tension built to an almost unbearable peak. By the time they pulled up in front of the drugstore her whole body was beginning to tremble.

"I'll be as quick as I can," she said.

Inside the store she went straight to the phone booth, dialed with care. Hugh himself answered and she was able to put her report in one sentence. He asked her present location, learned she was on her way to dinner at the Senator's house, and told her to delay her return to the car for five minutes. So her haste turned to waiting while her mind conjured up sirens, a rush of police and secret agents, a violent denouement in the middle of Wisconsin Avenue. When the five minutes were up it was an anticlimax to find the car just as she had left it.

The rest of the ride was uneventful. But when she was out of the car and on the Clayton porch she thought she saw a shadowy movement from the side of the garage into which the chauffeur was driving. By then her nervousness was controlled and she was able to return her hostess' greeting and embrace with no more unsteadiness of voice and body than was natural to her new bereavement. In the shelter of the Claytons' kindness she was able to put off fear and speculation through the simple but excellent meal. The coffee service was being taken from the living room when Mrs. Clayton was called to the phone.

"Jedediah," she said returning, "it's Mr. Pierce, the artist. You know him, don't you, Selena? A public-spirited citizen has commissioned him to paint the Senator's portrait to hang in the State Capitol. Isn't that splendid?"

"Only splendid thing," the Senator grumbled, "is that Pierce hasn't asked me to sit still for him."

"He was at the office most of the day, sketching while the Senator worked," Mrs. Clayton explained. "But he's worried about the jawline, so he's coming here for another look."

But when Hugh arrived, his clothes a little sprucer than those for neighborhood wear but his manner no less lethargic, Selena found her tension eased by the contrast between the Senator's gruff disavowal of interest and his effort to hold his head at an angle that would present an undoubled chin and jowl-less cheeks. In a few minutes Hugh nodded his satisfaction.

"I think I have it now," he said. "I appreciate your letting me interrupt your evening."

"No need to rush," the Senator protested.

"I have what I came for," he answered. "Since I'm going your way, Selena, can I offer you a ride?"

"You're not leaving so early, my dear? Grumman will drive you when you're ready to go."

"If you don't mind. I'm a little tired. It's been lovely being with you." She waited only till they were in his car. "They've arrested the chauffeur?"

"Yes. We sent two men to intercept him as he drove into the garage. He'd fixed the car intercom so it could be held open with the turn of a screw. Most of the time he left it closed—then he heard only what he was supposed to hear. But before he drove to the Hill in the afternoon he screwed it open. That's when the Senator was likely to give a lift to one of his colleagues and talk over what they'd heard in the committee room. The only way to catch him was to check the intercom right after the Senator got out. Your tip made that possible."

"I'm glad I helped. But you didn't need to drive out for me. At least, I assume that's why you came."

"Yes, the Senator's jaw was only a pretext. But I can't take credit for a courteous gesture. That's something we've no time for, I'm afraid. But when it's a question of handling a Senator with finesse, we have to make the time. If he'd learned that his chauffeur was missing when he tried to call him to take you home, he'd have been annoyed. We preferred that we get a carefully phrased report from one of our upper-echelon types. In fact—" he checked his watch "—he's speaking his piece right now. Everything had to be highly synchronized because we didn't want you there when he got the news. You'd have had to pretend surprise, shock, and various other emotions. So I came to personally pluck you from the nettle. Also, I'm curious to know your mode of operation."

"I began by doing as you asked—trying to remember every detail of those few minutes on Friday evening. The more I thought about it the more positive I was that the change in Simon came when he first caught sight of Senator Clayton. Then I realized that he didn't see just the Senator. The chauffeur was there too, holding the door. And it began to seem likely that that's what Simon was reacting to—that he must have recognized him from some other time and place."

"That's right. It was two years ago and in another country. Unfortunately, the recognition was mutual. He knew Simon had seen him and could tie him to his past. So he waited outside the Embassy and followed—but I won't go into that. You haven't explained how you knew about the intercom. When you phoned me you said, 'Senator Clayton thinks the back of his car is soundproof, but the driver hears every word that's spoken.' How could you be sure?"

"I asked the Senator to stop at a drugstore at Wisconsin and O, but when he switched on the box I gave the address as 1300 Wisconsin. That's actually a bank at Wisconsin and N—a block short. Yet the man drove directly to the O Street drugstore, so he must have heard me talking to the Senator while the box was turned off."

"Very simple." He took his eyes from the road to give her a swiftly appraising glance. "Also very clever and courageous. In our organization we've a high degree of cleverness, and abundance of courage. But this job called for another quality, one that only you could supply. We needed someone who's really in—someone who kicked sand at the Senator when she was a child. There'll be other jobs like that."

"This was a job that Simon left unfinished," she resisted. "Now it's done."

"One small piece is cleared away," he countered. "But the work Simon was doing is far from finished." He cut off her attempt to speak. "Some day, it may be soon, it may be a long time away, we'll need your special qualities. Then I'll ask you for a yes or no."

Citizen in Space

Robert Sheckley

I'm really in trouble now, more trouble than I ever thought possible. It's a little difficult to explain how I got into this mess, so maybe I'd better start at the beginning.

Ever since I graduated from trade school in 1991 I'd had a good job as sphinx valve assembler on the Starling Spaceship production line. I really loved those big ships, roaring to Cygnus and Alpha Centaurus and all the other places in the news. I was a young man with a future, I had friends, I even knew some girls.

But it was no good.

The job was fine, but I couldn't do my best work with those hidden cameras focused on my hands. Not that I minded the cameras themselves; it was the whirring noise they made. I couldn't concentrate.

I complained to Internal Security. I told them, look, why can't I have new, quiet cameras, like everybody else? But they were too busy to do anything about it.

Then lots of little things started to bother me. Like the tape recorder in my TV set. The F.B.I. never adjusted it right, and it hummed all night long. I complained a hundred times. I told them, look, nobody else's recorder hums that way. Why mine? But they always gave me that speech about winning the cold war, and how they couldn't please everybody.

Things like that make a person feel inferior. I suspected my government wasn't interested in me.

Take my Spy, for example. I was an 18-D Suspect—the same classification as the Vice-President—and this entitled me to part-time surveillance. But my particular Spy must have thought he was a movie actor, because he always wore a stained trench coat and a slouch hat jammed over his eyes. He was a thin, nervous type, and he followed practically on my heels for fear of losing me.

Well, he was trying his best. Spying is a competitive business, and I couldn't help but feel sorry, he was so bad at it. But it was embarrassing, just to be associated with him. My friends laughed themselves sick whenever I showed up with him breathing down the back of my neck. "Bill," they said, "is *that* the best you can do?" And my girl friends thought he was creepy.

Naturally, I went to the Senate Investigations Committee, and said, look, why can't you give me a *trained* Spy, like my friends have?

They said they'd see, but I knew I wasn't important enough to swing it.

All these little things put me on edge, and any psychologist will tell you it doesn't take something big to drive you bats. I was sick of being ignored, sick of being neglected.

That's when I started to think about Deep Space. There were billions of square miles of nothingness out there, dotted with too many stars to count. There were enough Earth-type planets for every man, woman, and child. There had to be a spot for me.

I bought a Universe Light List, and a tattered Galactic Pilot. I read through the Gravity Tide Book, and the Interstellar Pilot Charts. Finally I figured I knew as much as I'd ever know.

All my savings went into an old Chrysler Star Clipper. This antique leaked oxygen along its seams. It had a touchy atomic pile, and spacewarp drives that might throw you practically anywhere. It was dangerous, but the only life I was risking was my own. At least, that's what I thought.

So I got my passport, blue clearance, red clearance, numbers certificate, space-sickness shots, and deratification papers. At the job I collected my last day's pay and waved to the cameras. In the apartment I packed my clothes and said good-by to the recorders. On the street, I shook hands with my poor Spy and wished him luck.

I had burned my bridges behind me.

All that was left was final clearance, so I hurried down to the Final Clearance Office. A clerk with white hands and a sunlamp tan looked at me dubiously.

"Where did you wish to go?" he asked me.

"Space," I said.

"Of course. But where in space?"

"I don't know yet," I said. "Just space. Deep Space. Free Space."

The clerk sighed wearily. "You'll have to be more explicit than that, if you want a clearance. Are you going to settle on a planet in American Space? Or did you wish to emigrate to British Space? Or Dutch Space? Or French Space?"

"I didn't know *space* could be owned," I said.

"Then you don't keep up with the times," he told me, with a superior smirk. "The United States has claimed all space between coordinates 2XA and D2B, except for a small and relatively unimportant segment which is claimed by Mexico. The Soviet Union has coordinates 3DB to L02—a very bleak region, I can assure you. And then there is the Belgian Grant, the Chinese Grant, the Ceylonese Grant, the Nigerian Grant—"

I stopped him. "Where is Free Space?" I asked.

"There is none."

"None at all? How far do the boundary lines extend?"

"To infinity," he told me proudly.

For a moment it fetched me up short. Somehow I had never considered the possibility of every bit of infinite space being owned. But it was natural enough. After all, *somebody* had to own it.

"I want to go into American Space," I said. It didn't seem to matter at the time, although it turned out otherwise.

The clerk nodded sullenly. He checked my

records back to the age of five—there was no sense in going back any further—and gave me the Final Clearance.

The spaceport had my ship all serviced, and I managed to get away without blowing a tube. It wasn't until Earth dwindled to a pinpoint and disappeared behind me that I realized I wasn't alone.

Fifty hours out I was making a routine inspection of my stores, when I observed that one of my vegetable sacks had a shape unlike the other sacks. Upon opening it I found a girl, where a hundred pounds of potatoes should have been.

A stowaway. I stared at her, open-mouthed.

"Well," she said, "are you going to help me out? Or would you prefer to close the sack and forget the whole thing?"

I helped her out. She said, "Your potatoes are lumpy."

I could have said the same of her, with considerable approval. She was a slender girl, for the most part, with hair the reddish blond color of a flaring jet, a pert, dirt-smudged face, and brooding blue eyes. On Earth, I would gladly have walked ten miles to meet her. In space, I wasn't so sure.

"Could you give me something to eat?" she asked. "All I've had since we left is raw carrots."

I fixed her a sandwich. While she ate, I asked, "What are you doing here?"

"You wouldn't understand," she said between mouthfuls.

"Sure I would."

She walked to a porthole and looked out at the spectacle of stars —American stars, most of them —burning in the void of American space.

"I wanted to be free," she said.

"Huh?"

She sank wearily on my cot. "I suppose you'd call me a romantic," she said quietly. "I'm the sort of fool who recites poetry to herself in the black night, and cries in front of some absurd little statuette. Yellow autumn leaves make me tremble, and dew on a green lawn seems like the tears of all Earth. My psychiatrist tells me I'm a misfit."

She closed her eyes with a weariness I could appreciate. Standing in a potato sack for fifty hours can be pretty exhausting.

"Earth was getting me down," she said. "I couldn't stand it—the regimentation, the discipline, the privation, the cold war, the hot war, everything. I wanted to laugh in free air, run through green fields, walk unmolested through gloomy forests, sing—"

"But why did you pick on me?"

"You were bound for freedom," she said. "I'll leave, if you insist."

That was a pretty silly idea, out in the depths of space. And I couldn't afford the fuel to turn back.

"You can stay," I said.

"Thank you," she said very softly. "You *do* understand."

"Sure, sure," I said. "But we'll have to get a few things straight. First of all—" But she had fallen asleep on my cot, with a trusting smile on her lips.

Immediately, I searched her handbag. I found five lipsticks, a compact, a phial of Venus V perfume, a paper-bound book of poetry, and a badge that read: *Special Investigator, FBI.*

I had suspected it, of course. Girls don't talk that way, but Spies always do.

It was nice to know my government was still looking out for me. It made space seem less lonely.

The ship moved into the depths of American Space. By working fifteen hours out of twenty-four, I managed to keep my spacewarp drive in one piece, my atomic piles reasonably cool, and my hull seams tight. Mavis O'Day (as my Spy was named) made all meals, took care of the light housekeeping, and hid a number of small cameras around the ship. They buzzed abominably, but I pretended not to notice.

Under the circumstances, however, my relations with Miss O'Day were quite proper.

The trip was proceeding normally—even happily—until something happened.

I was dozing at the controls. Suddenly an intense light flared on my starboard bow. I leaped backward, knocking over Mavis as she was inserting a new reel of film into her number three camera.

"Excuse me," I said.

"Oh, trample me any time," she said.

I helped her to her feet. Her supple nearness was dangerously pleasant, and the tantalizing scent of Venus V tickled my nostrils.

"You can let me go now," she said.

"I know," I said, and continued to hold her. My mind inflamed by her nearness, I heard myself saying, "Mavis—I haven't known you very long, but—"

"Yes, Bill?" she asked.

In the madness of the moment I had forgotten our relationship of Suspect and Spy. I don't know what I might have said. But just then a second light blazed outside the ship.

I released Mavis and hurried to the controls. With difficulty I throttled the old Star Clipper to an idle, and looked around.

Outside, in the vast vacuum of space, was a single fragment of rock. Perched upon it was a child in a space suit, holding a box of flares in one hand and a tiny space-suited dog in the other.

Quickly, we got him inside and unbuttoned his space suit.

"My dog—" he said.

"He's all right, son," I told him.

"Terribly sorry to break in on you this way," the lad said.

"Forget it," I said. "What were you doing out there?"

"Sir," he began, in treble tones, "I will have to start at the start. My father was a spaceship test pilot, and he died valiantly, trying to break the light barrier. Mother recently remarried. Her present husband is a large, black-haired man with narrow, shifty eyes and tightly compressed lips. Until recently he was employed as a ribbon clerk in a large department store.

"He resented my presence from the beginning. I

suppose I reminded him of my dead father, with my blond curls, large oval eyes, and merry, outgoing ways. Our relationship smoldered fitfully. Then an uncle of his died (under suspicious circumstances) and he inherited holdings in British Space.

"Accordingly, we set out in our spaceship. As soon as we reached this deserted area, he said to Mother, 'Rachel, he's old enough to fend for himself.' My mother said, 'Dirk, he's so young!' But soft-hearted, laughing Mother was no match for the inflexible will of the man I would never call Father. He thrust me into my space suit, handed me a box of flares, put Flicker into his own little suit, and said, 'A lad can do all right for himself in space these days.' 'Sir,' I said, 'there is no planet within two hundred light years.' 'You'll make out,' he grinned, and thrust me upon this spur of rock."

The boy paused for breath and his dog Flicker looked up at me with moist oval eyes. I gave the dog a bowl of milk and bread, and watched the lad eat a peanut butter and jelly sandwich. Mavis carried the little chap into the bunk room and tenderly tucked him into bed.

I returned to the controls, started the ship again, and turned on the intercom.

"Wake up, you little idiot!" I heard Mavis say.

"Lemme sleep," the boy answered.

"Wake up! What did Congressional Investigation *mean* by sending you here? Don't they realize this is an FBI case?"

"He's been reclassified as a 10-F Suspect," the

boy said. "That calls for full surveillance."

"Yes, but *I'm* here," Mavis cried.

"You didn't do so well on your last case," the boy said. "I'm sorry, ma'am, but Security comes first."

"So they send you," Mavis said, sobbing now. "A twelve-year-old child—"

"I'll be thirteen in seven months."

"A twelve-year-old child! And I've tried so hard! I've studied, read books, taken evening courses, listened to lectures—"

"It's a tough break," the boy said sympathetically. "Personally, I want to be a spaceship test pilot. At my age, this is the only way I can get in flying hours. Do you think he'll let me fly the ship?"

I snapped off the intercom. I should have felt wonderful. Two full-time Spies were watching me. It meant I was really someone, someone to be watched.

But the truth was, my Spies were only a girl and a twelve-year-old boy. They must have been scraping bottom when they sent those two.

My government was still ignoring me, in its own fashion.

We managed well on the rest of the flight. Young Roy, as the lad was called, took over the piloting of the ship, and his dog sat alertly in the co-pilot's seat. Mavis continued to cook and keep house. I spent my time patching seams. We were as happy a group of Spies and Suspects as you could find.

We found an uninhabited Earth-type planet. Mavis liked it because it was small and rather cute, with the green fields and gloomy forests she had read about in her poetry books. Young Roy liked the clear lakes and the mountains, which were just the right height for a boy to climb.

We landed, and began to settle.

Young Roy found an immediate interest in the animals I animated from the freezer. He appointed himself guardian of cows and horses, protector of ducks and geese, defender of pigs and chickens. This kept him so busy that his reports to the Senate became fewer and fewer, and finally stopped altogether.

You really couldn't expect any more from a Spy of his age.

And after I had set up the domes and force-seeded a few acres, Mavis and I took long walks in the gloomy forest, and in the bright green and yellow fields that bordered it.

One day we packed a picnic lunch and ate on the edge of a little waterfall. Mavis's unbound hair spread lightly over her shoulders, and there was a distant enchanted look in her blue eyes. All in all, she seemed extremely un-Spylike, and I had to remind myself over and over of our respective roles.

"Bill," she said after a while.

"Yes?" I said.

"Nothing." She tugged at a blade of grass.

I couldn't figure that one out. But her hand strayed somewhere near mine. Our fingertips touched, and clung.

We were silent for a long time. Never had I been so happy.

"Bill?"

"Yes?"

"Bill dear, could you ever—"

What she was going to say, and what I might have answered, I will never know. At that moment our silence was shattered by the roar of jets. Down from the sky dropped a spaceship.

Ed Wallace, the pilot, was a white-haired old man in a slouch hat and a stained trench coat. He was a salesman for Clear-Flo, an outfit that cleansed water on a planetary basis. Since I had no need for his services, he thanked me, and left.

But he didn't get very far. His engines turned over once, and stopped with a frightening finality.

I looked over his drive mechanism, and found that a sphinx valve had blown. It would take me a month to make him a new one with hand tools.

"This is terribly awkward," he murmured. "I suppose I'll have to stay here."

"I suppose so," I said.

He looked at his ship regretfully. "Can't understand how it happened," he said.

"Maybe you weakened the valve when you cut it with a hacksaw," I said, and walked off. I had seen the telltale marks.

Mr. Wallace pretended not to hear me. That evening I overheard his report on the interstellar radio, which functioned perfectly. His home office, interestingly enough, was not Clear-Flo, but Central Intelligence.

* * * * *

Mr. Wallace made a good vegetable farmer, even though he spent most of his time sneaking around with camera and notebook. His presence spurred young Roy to greater efforts. Mavis and I stopped walking in the gloomy forest, and there didn't seem time to return to the yellow and green fields, to finish some unfinished sentences.

But our little settlement prospered. We had other visitors. A man and his wife from Regional Intelligence dropped by, posing as itinerant fruit pickers. They were followed by two girl photographers, secret representatives of the Executive Information Bureau, and then there was a young newspaper man, who was actually from the Idaho Council of Spatial Morals.

Every single one of them blew a sphinx valve when it came time to leave.

I didn't know whether to feel proud or ashamed. A half-dozen agents were watching *me*—but every one of them was a second-rater. And invariably, after a few weeks on my planet, they became involved in farmwork and the Spying efforts dwindled to nothing.

I had bitter moments. I pictured myself as a testing ground for novices, something to cut their teeth on. I was the Suspect they gave to Spies who were too old or too young, inefficient, scatter-brained, or just plain incompetent. I saw myself as a sort of half-pay retirement plan Suspect, a substitute for a pension.

But it didn't bother me too much. I did have a position, although it was a little difficult to define.

I was happier than I had ever been on Earth, and my Spies were pleasant and cooperative people.

Our little colony was happy and secure.

I thought it could go on forever.

Then, one fateful night, there was unusual activity. Some important message seemed to be coming in, and all radios were on. I had to ask a few Spies to share sets, to keep from burning out my generator.

Finally all radios were turned off, and the Spies held conferences. I heard them whispering into the small hours. The next morning, they were all assembled in the living room, and their faces were long and somber. Mavis stepped forward as spokeswoman.

"Something terrible has happened," she said to me. "But first, we have something to reveal to you. Bill, none of us are what we seemed. We are all Spies for the government."

"Huh?" I said, not wanting to hurt any feelings.

"It's true," she said. "We've been spying on you, Bill."

"Huh?" I said again. "Even you?"

"Even me," Mavis said unhappily.

"And now it's all over," young Roy blurted out. That shook me. "*Why?*" I asked.

They looked at each other. Finally Mr. Wallace, bending the rim of his hat back and forth in his calloused hands, said, "Bill, a resurvey has just shown that this sector of space is not owned by the United States."

"What country does own it?" I asked.

"Be calm," Mavis said. "Try to understand. This entire sector was overlooked in the international survey, and now it can't be claimed by our country. As the first to settle here, this planet, and several million miles of space surrounding it, belong to you, Bill."

I was too stunned to speak.

"Under the circumstances," Mavis continued, "we have no authorization to be here. So we're leaving immediately."

"But you can't!" I cried. "I haven't repaired your sphinx valves!"

"All Spies carry spare sphinx valves and hacksaw blades," she said gently.

Watching them troop out to their ships, I pictured the solitude ahead of me. I would have no government to watch over me. No longer would I hear footsteps in the night, turn, and see the dedicated face of a Spy behind me. No longer would the whirr of an old camera soothe me at work, nor the buzz of a defective recorder lull me to sleep.

And yet, I felt even sorrier for them. Those poor, earnest, clumsy, bungling Spies were returning to a fast, efficient, competitive world. Where would they find another Suspect like me, or another place like my planet?

"Good-by, Bill," Mavis said, offering me her hand.

I watched her walk to Mr. Wallace's ship. It was only then that I realized that she was no longer *my* Spy.

"Mavis!" I cried, running after her. She hurried toward the ship. I caught her by the arm. "Wait. There was something I started to say in the ship. I wanted to say it again on the picnic."

She tried to pull away from me. In most unromantic tones I croaked, "Mavis, I love you."

She was in my arms. We kissed, and I told her that her home was here, on this planet with its gloomy forests and yellow and green fields. Here with me.

She was too happy to speak.

With Mavis staying, young Roy reconsidered. Mr. Wallace's vegetables were just ripening, and he wanted to tend them. And everyone else had some chore or other that he couldn't drop.

So here I am—ruler, king, dictator, president, whatever I want to call myself. Spies are beginning to pour in now from *every* country—not only America.

To feed all my subjects, I'll soon have to import food. But the other rulers are beginning to refuse me aid. They think I've bribed their Spies to desert.

I haven't, I swear it. They just come.

I can't resign, because I own this place. And I haven't the heart to send them away. I'm at the end of my rope.

With my entire population consisting of former government Spies, you'd think I'd have an easy time forming a government of my own. But no, they're completely uncooperative. I'm the absolute ruler of a planet of farmers, dairymen, shepherds, and cattle raisers, so I guess we won't starve after all. But that's not the point. The point is: how am I supposed to rule?

Not a single one of these people will Spy for me.